TH
TRAH

Terence Blacker is one of a small number of authors who write for both adults and children. His many popular novels include the award-winning *Boy2Girl* and *ParentSwap*. He plays the guitar and writes songs, and lives in a house in the Suffolk countryside, which he converted from a goose hatchery.

Praise for *The Transfer*

'*The Transfer* is in a league of its own . . . a compulsively readable story . . . fantasy football as it should be'
*Sunday Telegraph*

'What a goal!'
*The Times*

'Sharp, funny and full of surprises'
*Mail on Sunday*

'This comic fantasy really hits the target . . . Blacker will be a huge hit with children as Nick Hornby has been with adults with *Fever Pitch*'
★★★★★*Books for Keeps*

'An ideal story for both football and computer fanatics . . . a great read'
*Bookseller*

# TERENCE BLACKER

# THE TRANSFER

MACMILLAN CHILDREN'S BOOKS

First published 1998 by Macmillan Children's Books

This edition published 2007 by Macmillan Children's Books
a division of Macmillan Publishers Limited
20 New Wharf Road, London N1 9RR
Basingstoke and Oxford
www.panmacmillan.com

Associated companies throughout the world

ISBN: 978-0-330-39786-5

5 7 9 8 6 4

A CIP catalogue record for this book is available from
the British Library.

Typeset by Intype Libra Ltd
Printed and bound in Great Britain by Mackays of Chatham plc, Kent

**Acknowledgement**
I would like to thank Tom Lloyd for his helpful and encouraging
comments on the manuscript of this novel.

*For Xan*

It's only a small paragraph on an inside page of the Sunday newspaper, but it catches my eye all right.

*Whatever happened to . . . LAZLO?*

Every week on this page they track down some former celebrity who has disappeared from the head-lines – the once-famous pop star who's now driving a van, the big-shot DJ who's sweeping roads, the glossy soap actress who's on the checkout till at a supermarket. Normally I skip it.

This week's different.

*Whatever happened to . . . LAZLO?*

There's a photograph of a footballer in a number 24 shirt, standing in front of a cheering crowd.

Only five years ago. History.

I open the kitchen drawer, take out a pair of scissors. There are some stories it would be better that my mum didn't read. Carefully, I cut around the article.

Upstairs, I go to my desk. Taking a key from my back pocket, I unlock the bottom drawer. Inside there's a folder. It's where I keep a few mementoes.

A ticket stub from the Liverpool game.

A calling card from *TERRY MILLS, Personal Management* with, scribbled on the back, 'Yo, guy – call me!'

An old piece of sticking plaster with the face of Popeye on the front.

And, already yellowing, a clutch of folded newspaper cuttings held together by a clip. I flick through them, every headline taking me back.

CRISIS CLUB IN MYSTERY TRANSFER

STRIKER SCORES IN NIGHTCLUB!

I WAS DUMPED BY LOVE-RAT LAZLO!

Then a smaller item from the local paper.

SCHOOLBOY FAN MISSING

Carefully, I attach the latest addition to the collection.

*Whatever happened to . . . LAZLO?*

The memories return . . .

# ONE

# CHAPTER I

## Peterson takes possession . . .

. . . in the middle of the school playground, during morning break. Unchallenged, he bounces the tennis ball first on his right foot, then his left . . .

. . . Looks for support, sees he's alone, takes it on himself. Rides one tackle, shimmies, rides another . . .

. . . He's just outside the area now. He flicks the ball up, heads it, holds it briefly on the back of his neck. He lets the ball bounce, turns and back-heels it over his head. This is incredible stuff. Now . . .

. . . Is he going to feed out to the right wing, or thread it through the defenders? He glances up, the ball's in the air, falling slowly, I don't believe it, he's going to . . .

. . . Peterson catches the ball with the sweetest half-volley you could ever imagine. The ball's heading for goal. It's got to be, it's going to be . . .

Crash!

*Oh dear, broken window. There's silence in the play-ground. They're all looking at him. Looks like yet another red card for . . .*

'Stanley Peterson.'

The headteacher Miss Boston sat back in her chair and gazed at me across her desk. She was quite a large woman, Miss Boston — when you saw her walking down the corridor, it was like watching a wardrobe on the move — and right now she looked larger than usual. She breathed in deeply, squaring her shoulders. The room seemed to get slightly darker.

'That's what I thought when I heard the sound of breaking glass.' She shook her head sorrowfully. 'That'll be Stanley Peterson.'

'I was practising my—'

'I know exactly what you were practising. You were practising football.'

I smiled. Sometimes just hearing that word makes me feel better. 'Yeah, football,' I said.

'It's good to have an interest,' she said, trying to be reasonable. 'But, Stanley, your interest is more than an interest. It's an obsession. You're not football-crazy. You're football-insane. You're football stark staring bonkers.'

*Peterson's facing up to Boston, the big defender.*

'I've asked Miss Tysoe for a report on your progress and for some examples of your work. She says you're bright enough . . .'

*Boston's towering over him.*

' . . . but when you do art, you draw a football pitch. When you do maths, you make the squares into goalnets.'

*He feints to the left. Boston's wrong-footed . . .*

'As for English . . .'

*He nutmegs her. Superb skills . . .*

'You even managed to bring football into Miss Tysoe's list of her favourite books. Look at this stuff. *Alice in the Premiership* by Lewis Carroll. *The Iron Man-to-Man Marker* by Ted Hughes. *James and the Giant Peach of a Goal* by Roald Dahl. *The Demon Header* by Gillian "Perfect" Cross.'

*He skips past Boston as if she weren't there, the goal's in his sights and—*

'Are you listening, Stanley?'

'Sorry, Miss Boston. I've got a lot on my mind.'

The headteacher put on her most sympathetic expression. 'Have you, Stanley? Is there something you'd like to share with me? Problems at home?'

'Not exactly.'

'Well? What's on your mind, Stanley?'

'It's City,' I said. 'I'm really, really worried about City.'

*We're part of a great wave — a wave of sound and feeling and hope.*

*City. Clap clap clap.*
*City. Clap clap clap.*
*City. Clap clap clap*

*Somewhere, from the other side of the ground, we can hear the other fans singing, 'Going down, going down, going down.'*

*We sing louder. If we can drown them out, maybe it won't be true. Surely no team with fans like us can be relegated.*

*We love you, City.*

*We do.*

'City. You're telling me your problem is the local football club.'

I tried to explain to Miss Boston about City. For ten years, they had been in the Premier League. Now, if they didn't win their last two games, they would be relegated. Next season, instead of playing Newcastle and Manchester United, it would be Grimsby and Southend. I had nothing against Grimsby or Southend but the thought of City playing them seemed all wrong. Unnatural.

'It's a game, Stanley,' said Miss Boston. 'It's sport.'

I shook my head. 'It's life,' I said. 'Ask anyone in my class.'

'Stanley—'

'And guess who our last two matches are against, Miss Boston.'

'Frankly, I don't—'

'Spurs, then Liverpool. At least they're both home games – but our home form's terrible.'

'Stanley—'

'In fact, we haven't scored more than two goals in any game this season.'

Miss Boston gave me the blankest of stares. 'It's time for you to snap out of this nonsense, Stanley Peterson. I've spoken to Mr O'Reardon to see whether you can train with the school team—'

'Back of the net!' I said. 'I mean, great.'

'He said you were too small to play in the team but he'll consider including you as a substitute in the John Sparks Cup the week after next against Chester Gardens. Maybe that will help get football out of your system. And I've written to your mother, explaining that I've given you a final warning.'

Final warning. All I could think of was the Cup Final. Only two seasons ago, City had reached the sixth round. And now we were facing the drop.

'Will you try to concentrate a bit more on school life?'

'Yes, Miss Boston,' I mumbled, adding under my breath, 'Just as soon as City manage to stay up.'

I went to the classroom where everyone was waiting for Miss Tysoe to arrive.

'All right?' said my friend Callan.

I shrugged and said, 'Nil–all draw', which is our way of saying something's dead boring. 'The head thinks I'm a bit too keen on football.'

'Yeah?' Callan went on doodling on the back of his exercise book.

'She's written a note to my mum.'

'Right.'

'Final warning.'

'I've been thinking.' Callan looked up at last. 'Maybe they should play Field at left back and shift Burton into midfield. He's good going forward, is Field. Down the left, to the byline, cross it to Georgie Dodd.'

'Back of the net!'

'Angie's worked out that, during the last ten seasons, three clubs who were second from bottom with two games to go managed to stay up.'

Angie, my other best friend, was at the next-door desk, trying to finish some homework she was meant to have done. '33.33 per cent chance of survival,' she said without looking up. 'But, taking into account City's lower goal differences, the odds fall to 23.5 per cent. Only one club in the last 25 years has made up a four-goal deficit in the last two games.'

I smiled at Callan. 'Thanks for clearing that up for us, Angie.'

As Miss Tysoe entered the class, the noise died down. She paused in front of my desk.

'I wonder what you three are talking about,' she said.

'We want Steve Malcolm to move Burton into midfield,' I said.

Miss Tysoe shook her head. 'You're a sad case, Stanley Peterson.'

'With Robbie Field at left back,' said Callan.

'Flat back four,' said Angie.

Miss Tysoe sighed. 'You are all completely crazy,' she said, walking slowly towards her desk. 'Anyone can see we need Budgie Burton's speed in defence.'

Maybe I am as football-crazy as Miss Boston said. But at least I'm not alone.

# CHAPTER 2

## There was a deathly silence . . .

. . . in the house when I got home that evening. The only sign of human occupation was a half-eaten pizza on the kitchen table. Whoever had been here hadn't finished that meal.

I went upstairs, step by step. The sound of a low hum was coming from the office at the top of the stairs. As I approached the door, I seemed to hear a sort of unearthly muttering. Slowly, I pushed the door open.

There was a figure sitting crouched in front of a computer, wearing on its head a sort of hairnet made of tiny electrical wires and metal terminals the size of small coins. The wires hung down at the back like a wedding veil. Slowly, the thing turned in its chair. It began to speak.

'Hi, Stan. I didn't hear you come in.'

'Hi, Mum.'

'Good day?'

I shrugged. 'Nil–all draw.'

She gave a sort of shudder. 'Is that better than "back of the net"?'

'It means boring, but all right.' I smiled innocently. Somehow it didn't seem the moment to mention the letter from Miss Boston which I had left on the hall table downstairs. 'How about you?'

My mother turned back to the monitor. In the centre of the screen was a picture of a small red car. She seemed to concentrate for a moment, narrowing her eyes. The car slowly changed from red to green.

'This morning I moved it, Stan,' she whispered. '1.3 centimetres. Left to right.'

'Go on then. Let's see you do it.'

'I'm too tired. It's been a tough day.'

'Oh yeah? Moving a little car on a screen?'

She laughed. 'Thanks, Stan. I knew you'd understand.'

I did understand, sort of. For as long as I could remember, Mum has been a computer scientist. When he lived here, Dad used to complain about the staring, blinking eye of the monitor with its occasional conversation of bleeps and whirrs. Why couldn't we have a pet like other families? he used to ask, half joking. Then Mum would give him one of her looks and he would fall quiet.

Dad was a freelance photographer but he was so unsuccessful that, for a long time, I thought that 'freelance' meant free of work. When Mum came back from the office, he used to go out, camera bag over his shoulder, and return hours later, often smelling of drink.

His dream was to be a sports photographer and, for a while, he was able to get into City games without paying. I remember watching him once from the stands, when I was at a game with Callan and his parents. Dad sat behind his camera on the byline near one of the goals. He was so absorbed in the game (City 3 Everton 2) that he didn't seem to take a single shot. Sometimes I wondered whether there was any film in his camera.

That was why Mum was able to silence him with a look. She was the one whose money kept us going. For as long as I remember, she had given up on him. She didn't believe in his work. She didn't believe in him.

And she hated football.

Over the years, City had come to stand for everything that she found disappointing in Dad. In fact, even my name had once been the subject of yet another great football row. Dad had wanted to call me Danny, after Danny O'Brien, the famous City striker of the early sixties. When Mum kicked that idea into touch, he had innocently suggested Stanley. Nice name, Mum thought. Only after I had been christened did he confess the truth.

Stanley Matthews. Stanley Bowles. And now Stanley Peterson. It was another football name.

That was probably his last victory. He left home when I was six. Over the past five years, he had drifted from job to job, from girlfriend to girlfriend, appearing now and then to take me to a game or away for a weekend. Mum sometimes referred to him as 'my mistake', 'the unmentionable' or (her favourite) 'the Dweeble'.

'By the way, the Dweeble rang for you.'

Mum had taken off her computer hairnet and we were in the kitchen. Frowning, she stabbed at a sausage as if it was Dad sizzling away in the frying pan.

'Wants to talk about some match on Saturday.'

'It's not some match, Mum. It's *the* match.'

'He said he'd ring later.' Mum paused and I knew what was coming next. 'That's the only thing he talks about with you.' She sighed. 'It's all his fault.'

I sat at the kitchen table, wanting to ask what exactly was his fault but, in my heart, I knew the answer. I was his fault – if it hadn't been for the Dweeble, I wouldn't be so crazy about City. There wouldn't be a letter from Miss Boston on the hall table. I wanted to tell her that my support for City was my decision, that these days it had nothing to do with Dad, but I knew from experience that now, at the end of the day when she was tired, was not the moment. I had to distract her mind from Dad, from my problems at school, from City. And there was only one sure way of doing that.

'I still don't understand what's so great about making that little car change colour and move a bit.'

'Can't you see, Stan? This is incredible . . .'

It worked. Waving the spatula in her hand around like a conductor, Mum began to talk about her research.

'What I'm doing is making something happen with the neurons in my brain. I'm taking the tiny electric currents generated by impulses in the brain, amplifying them hundreds of thousands of times and then digitizing them.'

'But why? I could get that car to move by using the mouse on the computer.'

'It started as an idea for people who were disabled. By tuning in to the alpha waves in their brains, what we called a mind-switch could turn on and off simple electrical things like a light or a kettle. But now I'm taking it further – extending the brain–body frequencies which the interface can recognize.'

'Which explains the hairnet, right?'

'Exactly. That headset places little electrodes against the brain-lobes. I'm changing the car's colour and moving it forward by the force of my will – making a direct connection between human intelligence and the intelligence of a machine. It's called "cybertelekinesis".'

When Mum starts talking about her work, a crazy, distant look comes into her eyes. She seems to forget where she is, that she's talking to her eleven-year-old son who has difficulty with long division, let alone alpha waves and weird cyberjunk. By now, she was so out of it that boiling fat from the spatula was flying through the air and smoke was rising from the sausages behind her.

'The only reason I can't do more is that my thoughts lack the kinetic power – my need to make the car move isn't strong enough. In the end, the brain is powered by something very simple – the human will.'

'So you have to really want something to happen to make it work.'

She smiled at me as if I was being unusually bright. 'That's right, Stan.'

'Like me wanting City to stay up, you mean.'

My mother's face changed, as it always does when I mention anything to do with football. She frowned and turned back to the cooker. 'Something like that,' she sighed.

# CHAPTER 3

## 'Hullo, son . . .

' . . . Ready for the big one on Saturday?'

'You bet, Dad. Hang on a second.' I pressed the mute button on the TV remote control and glanced across at Mum. She was asleep on the sofa, so I could relax and talk to my father about what was really on our minds. 'I think we can do it,' I said.

'With that joker Steve Malcolm in charge? Dream on.'

'He's all right, Dad. They've been playing better recently.'

'But not scoring. You can have the best defence in the league but, when you need points, you've got to win. And to win you need goals.'

'They'll do it. They can't go down.'

'It'll take a miracle. How's your mother?' Dad liked to throw this question into our conversations as if it was just a bit of passing-the-time-of-day politeness, but I was never fooled.

'Asleep,' I said.

'The work must be going well.' There was a smile in Dad's voice. 'In the old days, whenever she was working hard, she used to sit down in front of the evening news, glass of wine on the table beside her. One sip, news headlines and she was gone. Sometimes she fell asleep when I was talking to her.'

'She doesn't call it sleeping these days. She says it's a power nap.'

'Oh yeah?'

We both laughed a bit uneasily. Dad liked to pretend that being away from Mum and me was just fine, that bachelor life was great, but now and then I could hear the regret and anger in his voice. He couldn't admit that he was lonely. Mum couldn't admit that life was hard without him being around. I couldn't admit that I understood how they both felt. It was one of those family things.

'I think working on that computer does her head in,' I said. 'Sometimes she's so tired at the end of the day she can hardly talk.'

'Can't remember that bit,' said Dad, more coldly. 'I used to say that, if God had wanted us to move things with our brain, he wouldn't have given us hands.'

'Yeah.' This was one of Dad's favourite lines and even now I could remember how it used to annoy Mum. 'Are you going on Saturday?'

'I might have to take a rain check on that, son.'

'Does that mean no?'

'I was . . . meeting someone on Saturday.'

Hullo, here we go again. Dad's always meeting someone. The someone always seems to be female and a bit special. Then, a couple of weeks later, the someone has turned out not to be so special after all. Romantically, Dad's a bit of disaster area.

'Anyway, I couldn't stand the agony.' He sounded slightly embarrassed now. 'Seeing poor old City go down.'

'They might not. Miracles can happen.'

'Not at City they can't.' Dad's been disappointed so many times by our team that he has become a tad cynical.

'I'll give them a cheer for you then.'

'You do that, son.' He hesitated. 'And look after that power-napper.'

'I will. Bye, Dad.'

'Bye, son.'

I hung up and for a moment, watched the figures moving silently on the TV screen. They reminded me of Mum and the little car on the computer upstairs.

*You have to really want something to happen to make it work . . . It'll take a miracle to save City . . .* I shook my head, trying to clear it of the dangerous thoughts that were occurring to me.

But there was no escaping them. After a few seconds, I decided to let fate decide.

If my mother woke up now, I wouldn't go upstairs.

'Mum,' I said out loud.

She murmured to herself, then turned over on the sofa and started snoring gently.

If the computer was switched off, then I would forget about my little experiment.

I stood up, and made my way up the stairs. I hesitated outside the office door. I pushed the door open.

# CHAPTER 4

## The computer was switched on . . .

. . . and I stood in front of the blue screen, as if already I was aware that something weird and momentous was about to happen.

Will-power. The ability to make things happen with the strength of my own need. What did City need in order to stay up? I reached for a rack of computer games that lay on a nearby shelf. I flicked through the disks until I found what I wanted. What did City need? I slipped one of my favourite games into the computer. *TargetMan*.

I had no idea what would happen if I brought together Mum's research with the *TargetMan* computer game, but someone had to save City. Someone had to risk all.

*It's a penalty and Peterson's going to take it! At this*

*stage of the game, it's all about character and this brilliant young player has elected to step up and risk all on behalf of his team.*

I sat in the chair in front of the computer, then, taking a deep breath, I clicked on to *TargetMan*.

*The ball's on the spot. Peterson turns. The stadium has fallen silent. He starts his run-up . . .*

I accessed the superhero I had been working on – a striker with the skills of Maradona, the power of Pele, the vision of Bobby Charlton, the goal instinct of Lineker. I had called him Lazlo. He stood in the centre of the screen, a small computer graphic bouncing a tiny white football on his right foot.

My heart thumping, I reached for Mum's electronic headband. I slipped it carefully over my head and tightened the strap, until I felt the electrodes cool against my scalp.

I gazed at the screen and thought of City. There was a brief flash on the screen as if a power surge was working through the system.

'Back of the net,' I whispered.

I concentrated on Lazlo.

Lazlo of the City.

The yellow of his strip turned to the red and white squares of City.

'Welcome to City Stadium, Mr Lazlo,' I whispered.

Without my even having another thought, a panel had appeared on the monitor. It read:

PLAYER PROFILE:
POSITION?

I thought, *Striker*. The screen asked:

TALENT RATING OUT OF TEN:
BALL SKILLS?

*Ten*.

SPEED?

*Ten*.

GOAL–SCORING ABILITY?

*Ten*. This was easy.

POSITIONAL SENSE?

*Ten*.

PHYSICAL STRENGTH?

Again, I thought, *Ten*, but this time a message appeared on the screen: LAZLO HAS ONLY TEN TALENT POINTS REMAINING.

I shrugged. *Five.*

HEIGHT?

*Five.*

BLINK TO CONFIRM PLAYER PROFILE

I blinked.

No longer nervous or afraid, I felt at one with the computer. Lazlo was a City player, the dream striker that would save them from relegation. At another time, I might have worried about how a game could become reality, how a tiny computer figure could save a real team but, for some reason, I had no doubt. Will-power would find a way.

I was wondering what to do next when something odd happened. The figure on the monitor seemed to change. He grew larger, more lifelike. He began to do stretching exercises, as if he were warming up for a game.

Another panel appeared. PLAYER MISSION?

I hesitated. As if it understood my confusion, the computer asked, WHAT MISSION DO YOU WISH LAZLO TO ACHIEVE?

I felt tired now, and a strange fuzzy ache seemed to fill my skull, but I gathered what strength there was left in my brain. *Save the City.*

VIRTUAL REALITY?

'No,' I said out loud. *Real reality.*

The monitor changed again. Lazlo had moved closer, so that I could only see his face and shoulders as he stared out at me from the screen. He had a thin face, like me, slightly sticking-out ears, a bit like me, his hair was dark and untidy, a bit like mine. I noticed that he had a small scar in his left eyebrow, a bit like mine. In fact, exactly like mine.

Uh-oh.

I moved to the left. Lazlo moved too. I reached out my hand. He seemed to reach out for me.

My mouth was dry. I was having difficulty breathing. I swallowed, licked my lips. So did Lazlo.

I was staring at a grown-up version of myself.

*What's happening?*

A message appeared across the bottom of the screen.

AFFIX THE STUD
WHEN IT MAKES CONTACT, YOU ARE LAZLO

*I'm* Lazlo?

I was frightened now, breathing heavily. My mum had warned me never to touch the headset. I had always thought she was afraid of my messing up her programme. Now, for the first time, I realized that I was meddling with something beyond my control.

I took off the electronic hairnet. As soon as the electrodes lost contact with my skin, which now slick with sweat, the screen returned to normal

*TargetMan* mode, with a tiny Lazlo bouncing his little computer football again.

As I laid it on the table, something fell from the headband on to the wooden floor. I closed my eyes in horror — Mum's precious hairnet was coming apart in my hands. I was dead.

Dreading what I would see, I opened my eyes again. There, still spinning slowly on the floor, was a bright red plastic control button. I reached down and picked it up carefully. I looked more closely.

It wasn't a control button at all . . .

# CHAPTER 5

## It was a football stud . . .

. . . and it was steaming slightly as it lay, warm in the palm of my hand. I slipped it into my pocket.

I went downstairs in a daze. My head felt heavy on my shoulders as if my brain had turned into a lump of old stale dough. If it hadn't been for the football stud which seemed to glow in my trouser pocket, I might have put down the events of the previous few minutes to a particularly strange dream.

Lazlo. Saviour of the City. *Affix the stud*. What did that mean?

Before me, on the hall table, lay the headteacher's letter. Reality. Without thinking, I picked it up and took it into the sitting room.

'Mum? Miss Boston wrote to you.'

My mother opened her eyes. She took the letter. 'Now what?' She groaned as she opened it.

'I broke a window.'

She scanned the letter quickly. From the look on her face I could tell it wasn't exactly a rave review.

'What were you doing?' asked Mum.

'A left-footed half-volley from the edge of the box.'

Mum closed her eyes. 'I wouldn't have minded if it was anything else – rave music, gambling on the lottery, girlfriends. But football.' She buried her head under a cushion.

'It's City,' I said. 'If only . . .'

Mum took the cushion off her head and sat up like someone who has been told that she must behave like a grown-up parent. 'I don't want to hear another word about City or football or midfield generals or flat back fours or sweepers or strikers. You can go to all the games you want but, when you're at school, concentrate on school.'

'City.' The words came from me in a zombie croak. Before my eyes, I seemed to see the figure of Lazlo staring at me from the screen. I felt tired to the marrow of my bones.

'Are you all right, Stanley?' Mum asked. 'You've gone terribly pale.'

'I think I'll go to bed.'

'Bed?' Mum looked surprised. 'It's only eight o'clock.'

'I'm beat.' I leant forward and she kissed me, then felt my forehead.

31

'Bit warm,' she said. 'Hope you're not coming down with something.'

Minutes later, I lay in bed, staring at the ceiling, listening to the pounding of my blood, like a deep bass guitar. I reached under the pillow for the stud. It was still warm, as if glowing from an inner energy. I fell asleep, still holding it in my palm.

The next thing I knew was that it was the middle of the night. The room was dark, lit only by the street lamp shining through a crack between the curtains. I felt weirdly, unnaturally wakeful.

Had I been scared into consciousness by a dream? No. I remembered dreams. This was something else.

Then, sticking into my shoulder, glowing through my pyjamas, I felt the stud and knew what had woken me.

I got out of bed and quietly opened the door. Sometimes Mum worked late, but the computer room was dark and the sound of rhythmic breathing could be heard coming from her room.

I closed the bedroom door and walked to the cupboard where I kept my sports kit. I took out my football boots, then felt in the pocket of the bag for the small plastic key for unscrewing the studs. Slowly, I removed a stud from the right boot.

I put both boots on my feet, then hobbled over to the bed.

AFFIX THE STUD.

The words from the computer seemed to echo in my head like a distant command.

I sat on the bed, took a deep breath. I picked up the red stud and put it in the place of the missing stud on my right boot. It was a perfect fit.

I turned the stud key.

Nothing happened.

Turn.

Nothing.

Turn . . .

Tighten.

A blinding flash exploded in front of my eyes and a sort of eruption from within me threw me back on to the bed. For what seemed like minutes, but was probably no more than ten seconds, my body was convulsed as if an incredibly powerful electrical current was passing through me, then – as instantly as it began – it cut out.

I was on my back, my breath coming to me in sobbing gasps. When I slowly opened my eyes, the bedroom ceiling was blurry and indistinct. I reached up to wipe away the tears with the back of my hand.

The back of my hand was changed. It was covered with a forest of dark, wiry hairs. The hand itself seemed to have swollen to twice its normal size.

I blinked, tried to shake myself awake, then looked down.

My body seemed to go on for ever. Instead of pyjama tops, I was wearing a football shirt. Red and white. The City strip.

33

No. This couldn't be. I raised my right leg.

It was massive. The matchstick I was used to seeing had became a great dark-haired treetrunk. I touched my face. My chin was rough with stubbly hair.

'Noooo.' The groan that came from me was low and throaty, like the growl of a sleeping lion. I tried it again. 'It's true.'

The words were mine, but they were spoken in an odd foreign accent.

Slowly, I stood up and walked to the mirror. 'I'm Stanley Peterson,' I murmured in my strange new voice. 'I'm Stanley.'

But I wasn't. Staring back at me from the mirror was a dark, small, powerfully built footballer – a footballer that I had last seen on a computer screen. I turned slowly. On the back of my shirt was the number 24 and a name. Even in the reflection, I could see that the name was *Lazlo*.

It was at that moment that the full terror of the situation hit me. I wanted Stanley back – now. Panicking, I grabbed the key which was lying on the bed, undid the laces on my right boot, took it off, and turned the red stud.

There was no flash this time. Only a strange, slow swishing, like the sound of wet tyres on tarmac. I fell back on the bed, squeezing my eyes shut, clenching my fists. Someone somewhere was shouting, calling for his mother. I was trapped, struggling.

'Stanley! *Stanley!*'

34

I opened my eyes to find myself writhing at the end of the bed. My mother's arms were trying to restrain me.

'It's all right, darling,' she was saying. 'It's all right.'

I looked down. I was wearing my pyjamas. My hands and legs were back to their normal, skinny selves. I held on to Mum. 'I had this terrible dream,' I whispered.

'What was it about, for heaven's sake? You're shaking.'

I was about to tell her about the stud, about Lazlo, the whole crazy nightmare, when I noticed she was staring at my feet.

'Why are you wearing a football boot, Stanley?' she asked.

# CHAPTER 6

## I walked slowly . . .

. . . to school the next morning, my mind full of the events of the night. Suddenly all the gossip and chat and worry about City seemed like a pointless waste of energy. My mind had emptied itself of the jangle of everyday distractions. I was filled with a purpose which at that moment I couldn't quite understand. I felt as if I was walking towards Saturday.

Angie ran up as I entered the playground. 'I rang Club Call last night,' she said. 'Deano's back to full fitness. I worked out that City have only lost 17.5 per cent of their matches this season when he's been playing.'

'Great.'

'And we've only been beaten twice by Spurs in the last five seasons when he was in central defence. He's our lucky player.'

'Right.'

'Where's your tennis ball?'

'Mm? Oh, I left it at home.' I walked ahead of Angie into the school building.

'What's wrong with you today?' she called after me.

I hesitated, wondering for an instant whether to tell her about Lazlo and everything that had happened last night. But no – Angie was a fact person. Stories about magic studs and computer characters taking over my body would just convince her that the strain of supporting City had finally got to me. 'I'm fine,' I said. 'Why?'

'You seem different. Not your normal self.'

I was different. I felt strong and focused; yet distantly aware of a strange sense of anticipation – the sort of feeling you have before a really important test or exam.

During the first lesson that morning, Miss Tysoe walked into the classroom and asked us to write a story. Usually, I'd try to include a secret football message in my work – tell a story about a gunner who lived in a villa deep in the city, who finds these spurs in the heart of a forest – but today I just wrote my composition without a single mention of a football team.

'This is good, Stanley.' Miss Tysoe glanced over my shoulder as I worked. 'You actually seem to have listened to what somebody told you and forgotten about City.'

'They're always at the back of my mind,' I said.

'At the back of his mind and at the bottom of the league.' Matthew, a Manchester United fan, laughed, then began to sing mockingly, 'Going down with the City, down with the City, down with the—'

I turned to look at him. Something in my expression seemed to shut him up.

'I don't think so,' I said quietly.

It was later that day that I received my biggest shock.

I was walking home with Callan and we called in at a shop to buy a few sweets. As we waited to be served, Callan picked up an evening paper. Splashed across the back page was the headline STEVE SPRINGS BIG MATCH SURPRISE.

Callan read the story to me. 'City manager Steve Malcolm has named a mystery foreign player in his squad for Saturday's big relegation clash against Spurs. "We've been keeping quiet about this lad Lazlo," Malcolm told reporters at the City stadium. "He's a signing we made a few months ago but one we have the highest hopes for." '

Callan put down the paper. 'Lazlo?'

# CHAPTER 7

## Who on earth is Lazlo . . .?

. . . That was the question on the back pages of all the newspapers over the next two days.

Some reporters said that he had been seen playing for the Reserves. Others said that he would have played for City before now but his work permit had taken time to come through. Where was he from? A Lazlo had been found who had once played for the Rumanian side, Steaua Bucharest, but then it was discovered that he had retired four years ago. A rumour spread that none of the City players had met Lazlo, that maybe he had been invented by the manager Steve Malcolm in order to put psychological pressure on Spurs before Saturday's game.

There was even a report – surely this couldn't be true – that the words 'Lazlo, striker' had just appeared this very week on the City computer's team list and that, desperately short of anyone who could score a goal, the manager had included him in the squad.

One thing was sure. Malcolm was giving nothing away. 'Lazlo? No comment,' he told reporters again and again.

There had never been any doubt that the game at City Stadium was going to be one of Saturday's big matches. Win or lose, Spurs would be among the League's top five teams and would be playing in Europe next season, but if City lost, they were relegated. And the Lazlo story added a touch of mystery to the drama.

In some of the newspapers, there were comparisons of the teams' strikers – and it didn't exactly make reassuring reading for the average City fan. Gibson and White of Spurs had scored 37 goals between them this season. Georgie Dodd and Kevin Miller, City strike force, had scored . . . 14.

Which brought the discussion back to Lazlo . . .

Late that Saturday morning, Callan and Angie came round to my house. As usual, they were both dressed head-to-toe in City colours. As usual, my mother gave us lunch early so that we could leave early for the game.

'If you three worried half as much about your work as you did about that blinkin' game, you'd have no problems at all,' she said as we all sat in the kitchen. 'Stanley's so football-crazy that he's even started acting like a footballer.'

Callan and Angie looked at me curiously.

'He's doing stretching exercises in his bedroom every morning,' Mum continued. 'And insisting on eating nothing but pasta and salad.'

I shrugged. 'Pasta's what you should eat when you're in training. That's what all the best players say.'

'But, excuse me, you're not actually playing, Stan,' said Angie.

'I'm in training as a fan. We've got a tough afternoon ahead of us.'

'He's been acting pretty weird at school,' said Callan. 'He hardly talks these days. He's got an odd look in his eyes.'

My mother put a big bowl on the kitchen table. 'I'm beginning to see what Miss Boston's worried about,' she said, ladling some spaghetti onto my plate. 'Football sends people mad.'

'Not too much pasta, Mum,' I said. 'It'll blunt my speed.'

The three of them laughed.

I didn't.

How was I feeling? Strange. Tense. Two days ago, I had worried about what I should do. Part of me clung on to the past, told me that changing into a short, hairy adult was dangerous and stupid, that I should just chuck the red stud and forget anything had happened. Be what I was born to be. A fan.

But then, quite quickly, I began to feel different and the worries faded. I may have looked and talked and sounded like Stanley Peterson but inside, I knew, I had become Lazlo. I had a job to do. There was no choice.

I finished lunch quickly and told Angie and Callan that I wanted to get to the ground early. They understood — we all liked to soak up the atmosphere in the stands before a big game, watch the players warming up, hear the fans practising their chants.

Explaining the plastic bag I was taking with me was a bit more difficult.

'Your football boots?' said Mum, looking in the bag as we prepared to go.

'They're lucky,' I said lamely. 'A sort of mascot.'

'You'll lose them.' My mother tried to take the bag from me.

I fixed her with my new cool stare. 'I need them,' I said quietly.

She shrugged and let go. 'There's no need to be aggressive,' she muttered.

The twenty-minute walk to the ground passed in a haze. I found it more and more difficult to chat normally. When Angie asked me why I was jogging every few steps, I replied without thinking that I was warming up.

Callan made a joke but I wasn't listening.

There was a bad moment just after we entered the ground. It was an hour and a half before kick-off but already people were drifting into the family stand.

We walked through the turnstile. Two security men were waiting. One of them asked to see my bag.

He took out one of the boots and smiled coldly. 'Playing in the game, are we?' he asked.

I went for a white lie. 'Came straight from practice,' I said.

He nodded in the direction of the turnstile. 'Leave them with the steward,' he said. 'You can collect them after the game.'

'No!' My voice was louder than I meant to be. 'I mean, sorry but, please, no.'

'They're his lucky boots,' said Callan.

'And City need all the luck they can get.' Angie smiled sweetly.

'We've been warned there might be trouble at the game.' The security officer looked bored with the discussion.

'He's not exactly going to throw his best boots on to the pitch,' said Callan.

I smiled and tried to make myself look particularly pathetic and innocent. 'Please, sir,' I said in a small voice.

'Lucky boots.' Laughing, the man pushed the bag back into my hand. 'They'll need more than a pair of lucky boots, this lot.'

We were in. It was time for the moment of truth.

'I'll join you in a minute,' I said, as Callan and

Angie climbed the steps into the stand. 'I need to go to the toilet.'

'Already?' Angie frowned. 'You just went at the house.'

'Big match nerves.'

They turned to go.

'If I'm late back to my seat, don't worry,' I blurted out. 'I . . . might try to get a seat nearer the pitch.'

Before they could say anything, I was gone.

Later, just before kick-off or at half-time, the gents' toilets would be heaving with life, with fans joking as they queued. But now it was empty.

I made for a cubicle and locked the door behind me.

I took off my trainers, opened the plastic bag, took out the boots and put them on.

Then, more slowly, I reached into the pocket of my City tracksuit. The red stud was in the palm of my hand.

I hesitated for a moment. Then I laid my left foot on my right knee. I placed the stud in the empty socket.

'Go for it, Lazlo,' I whispered.

I turned the stud.

# CHAPTER 8

## 'Are you all right in there . . .?'

. . . The voice came from far away. I opened my eyes slowly to find I was looking under the door of the cubicle. The stone floor felt cold against my cheek.

I groaned – the low rumble from the base of my throat that I now recognized. I touched my chin. Rough, stubbly.

Now I was awake.

Someone knocked nervously on the door. 'You OK, mate?'

I stood up slowly, looked down at the red, white and blue strip. The shorts. The powerful legs. The boots.

I wasn't me any more. I was Lazlo.

I took off the shirt, trying to ignore the great

forest of black hair on my chest, and turned it over. It read:

## 24
## LAZLO

I put the shirt back on and took several deep breaths. It wasn't the most glamorous of starting places – a toilet under the Family Stand – but it was time for Lazlo to make his entrance.

At my feet lay my trainers and the plastic bag in which I had carried my boots. Stuffing them behind the toilet, I turned, then drew back the bolt on the door.

A short bald man wearing last season's City strip stood in front of me, a boy of about seven or eight hovering nervously behind him. 'There was a hell of a crash in there, mate,' he said. 'Thought someone was having a heart attack.'

It was the moment of truth – the first of many moments of truth. Could Lazlo talk?

'I'm fine.' I gave him a thumbs-up sign. 'Back of the net.'

The words were mine but the voice was deep and gruff. My accent made me sound like someone being sick.

The man and his son watched in amazement as I made my way out of the toilet, the sound of my studs echoing on the stone floor with every step.

'Dad,' I heard the little boy whisper. 'It's Lazlo!'

Ignoring the stares of the fans, I made my way to

the entrance of the family stand. But instead of going up to the back of the stand where Callan and Angie would be sitting, I walked down to the front seats and, without a second's hesitation, stepped over the low wall between the stand and the pitch.

At the far end of the ground, three City players – Dodd, Dean and Field – were warming up, taking occasional shots at Peters in goal.

I jogged for a few yards, then decided to test Lazlo's speed. As I accelerated, a surge of power coursed through my body – I was covering the ground at the speed and power of a sports car. I slowed, then sprinted again. Suddenly, all my worries about relegation, about the match, about Stanley and Lazlo, seemed to lift off my shoulders. I had total confidence. I knew what I had to do. I could achieve anything.

As I approached the edge of the pitch to sprint back again, I became aware of a group of officials standing by the dug-out. There was Joe Smith, the youth team manager, and a couple of the injured players. I smiled at them briefly then did a few standing jumps, as if heading an invisible ball.

Rocket launch! I rose, then seemed to hang in the air for a second or two before coming down.

I looked back at the bench. Someone had fetched Steve Malcolm. I saw the familiar tall, long-haired figure of the City manager staring at me. He beckoned. I jogged towards him.

Malcolm guided me away from the group of

staring City officials so that we were standing alone.

'What's your game, sonny?'

'Football,' I said simply. 'My name's Lazlo.'

He narrowed his eyes. 'All right, 'op it. I'm not in the mood for practical jokes.'

'It's not a joke, Mr Malcolm. I'm on your books, right?'

The manager shrugged. 'There is a Lazlo there. Don't know how it got there – I some kind of glitch on the computer probably.'

'Trust me. I can score goals.'

'You don't know me, son.' Malcolm lowered his voice. 'If there's one thing I don't like, it's people taking the mick.'

'I'm not. Just give me a chance to show you what I can do.'

He pursed his lips as if he had made a decision. 'I don't know what's going on here, Mr . . . Lazlo, but if it's some kind of stunt, there's going to be big trouble.' He nodded in the direction of the goal. 'Go out there and take a few shots at goal.'

He turned to Joe Smith. The two men spoke quietly, then Smith picked up the netful of practice balls that were by the dug-out.

Smith looked at me suspiciously. 'You speaky ze English?' he said.

'No problems.'

'Me cross the ball from the byline. You score ze goal. Comprende?'

I smiled. It wasn't the moment to tell him he

didn't have to speak in a silly accent to make me understand. 'Yeah, comprende,' I said.

Smith had a word with the three players. Dodd and Field ran to the far touchline while Joe Smith and Bill Dean trotted to the near corner flag.

'You scorey goaly,' Smith called over his shoulder, pointing to the sixteen-yard box.

I nodded and took up position. 'Scorey goaly, eh?' I murmured to myself. 'Goaly coming up.'

Gary Peters, the 6'4" keeper, called out to me. 'What's going on? Who the hell are you?'

'Lazlo,' I shouted. 'I'm taking shots.' Before I could explain any further, the first ball came in from the left.

It was not really a cross – more like an insultingly gentle lob. I took it on my right foot, tapped it up and struck it with as much force as I could with my left. As it hit the top of the crossbar, the clunk of leather on wood echoed around the ground as the ball rocketed into the stands behind the goal. It had been travelling so fast that Gary Peters had hardly moved as it passed him.

Dodd sent one in low and hard from the other side. This one I hit first time with the outside of my right foot. It swerved beyond the flailing hands of the goalkeeper into the top left hand corner of the goal.

Joe Smith hit an awkward high cross. Instinctively I leapt, nodding the ball across the goalmouth. It crept under the crossbar.

They speeded up the delivery, sending in every kind of ball, but I had my range now. Again and again I beat the keeper whose face had darkened with quiet anger and determination.

Although only a few fans were in the seats behind the goal, I sensed a quickening of interest, hands pointing, people standing in the aisles unable to believe what they were seeing.

Field was jogging towards me. ''Ere, Lazlo, or whatever your name is,' he called out. 'Now you've got to beat a defender and score.' He stood between me and the goal.

The next cross was a bad one – too short to reach me and with no power on it. I sprinted to meet the ball, did a little dummy, back-heeled and turned. As Field tried to regain his balance, I took the ball early, hitting low and hard. It crept into goal, bouncing off a sidepost.

A couple more came in. Both times I left the defender for dead. Field, one of the best man-markers in the Premier League, was no match for Lazlo.

At a signal from Steve Malcolm, we made our way back to the dug-out. Ahead of me, I heard the City players muttering, glancing in my direction. Field and Peters attempted to ignore me. I had made them look stupid. I'd need to win them back on to my side. As the team walked down the tunnel, Malcolm called me over.

'I don't know who you are or where you come from, Mr Lazlo – we'll sort that out after the game. Until then, just play this my way, right? Keep your mouth shut whatever I might say to the lads.'

'Am I in the team?'

'You're joking, son. You don't just turn up and walk into the City team.'

My shoulders sagged with disappointment.

'You're on the bench.' Malcolm gave me a look which seemed almost angry. 'Substitute.'

I smiled. 'Back of the net.'

'Boss,' said the manager.

'Sorry?'

'Back of the net, boss.'

'Back of the net, boss,' I said.

Some small voice at the back of my head was telling me that this was the strangest, most exciting thing that had ever happened to me. I was walking beside the one and only Steve Malcolm. Four of the players whose photographs were on my bedroom wall were walking ahead of me. Somewhere in the family stand – I glanced over my shoulder – Callan and Angie would be worrying about me. I was on the substitutes' bench in one of the biggest games in City's history.

But that voice was becoming quieter by the second. I no longer felt like Stanley Peterson in disguise. When the keeper Gary Peters looked coldly over his shoulder at me, I didn't blush or look away or think about asking him for his autograph. I stared straight back, player to player, then nodded coolly. He looked away.

Ahead of us was a door marked *Home Team*. I followed the manager and the four players into a brightly lit dressing room. The rest of the team were sitting on the benches around the room. Some were rubbing liniment on their legs or doing warm-up exercises.

The manager stood in the centre of the room and suddenly there was silence. All eyes were on me as I stood beside him.

'Team change,' he said calmly. 'For certain reasons, I've been holding back information concerning a new signing.' He placed a hand on my shoulder. 'This is Lazlo,' he said. 'He'll be on the bench instead of Sturgess.'

I winced inwardly. Martin Sturgess was one of the oldest players at City, and one of the most popular. Over the last month he had returned to the first team after a series of injuries. Although he hadn't scored any goals and was a bit slow these days, he was a big favourite with the fans.

'We're used to playing with Martin, boss.' Dean spoke up. 'He's been looking great on the training ground.'

'Yeah, if Martin comes on, he'll give us a bit of height,' said Kevin Miller, with a glance in my direction.

'This is not for discussion.' Malcolm glanced at his watch. 'I'll see you after the warm-up.'

I was left with the players. When we had arrived in the changing room, the atmosphere had seemed tense. Now it was angry. I looked around me for a friendly face but was met with stony stares. Sturgess swore and spat on the ground.

I noticed a corner where no one was sitting and made my way there.

OK, so they didn't trust me – didn't even like me. It was not my problem.

I had a match to win.

# CHAPTER 9

## Above our heads . . .

. . . we heard, growing louder by the minute, the chants of the fans. All the fuss surrounding the game was now part of an outside world of talk and headlines and gossip. Now only the game mattered. Nothing else even existed.

Now and then, as we waited in the changing room for the manager to return, one of the other lads spoke, passing the time, cracking a joke, but I could tell that they felt the same way, too. At one point, I noticed Billy Dean watching me. I gave him a cool Lazlo smile.

The door opened and, as if at a signal, the team stood up.

'Right, lads.' Steve Malcolm walked in and closed the door behind him. 'This is the big one.'

For a minute or so, he reminded them of the tactics and set pieces they had worked on in training.

He talked through the defence, the midfield formation, then paused when he came to the strike force. 'Kevin, Georgie.' He turned to the two attackers. 'It's all about goals today. We can turn in the best team performance of the season but, if you don't stick it in the back of the net, we're as good as down. A nil–all draw means we have to beat Liverpool by four clear goals – which we will not do. Remember . . .' He glanced in my direction. 'We've got old Geronimo here on the bench.'

I smiled politely at the joke.

Moments later, we were following him down the tunnel and forming up beside the Spurs team, one or two of the players nodding briefly in recognition of friends. Others jogged nervously. I stared straight ahead. The steward called us forward.

As we emerged from the tunnel, briefly dazzled by the spring sunlight, the roar of anticipation from the fans seemed to buffet the air around us. We jogged on to the pitch, sprinting to the Loft end where our fans were gathered. The warm-up period passed in a flash. I walked back to the dug-out where Joe Smith pointed to a seat behind the manager. 'I've got a feeling we'll be needing you, sunshine,' he muttered, as if he were talking to himself rather than me.

The teams moved into position. A tense silence descended on the stadium. Then, as the whistle blew, a roar of expectation seemed to vibrate in the air.

I thought of Steve Malcolm's words. The big one.

★

The first half seemed to pass in no time. It was a typical City performance – stylish, skilful, committed. Apart from one scare, when the Spurs striker Gibson wrong-footed Deano, was one-on-one with Peters and pulled his shot wide, the defence looked solid. Our young winger, his dreadlocks flying behind him, was tearing them apart down the right. Burton and Stringer were winning everything in midfield.

Stylish, skilful, committed – and yet going nowhere. City fans had seen it all before.

It wasn't that Georgie Dodd and Kevin Miller weren't working hard up front. Yet, whenever the Spurs goalmouth was at their mercy, a terrible anxiety seemed to grip them, as if each of them knew that, with a swing of a boot, they could change people's lives. So they swung – and sent the ball soaring over the bar, or towards the corner flag, or into the keeper's arms.

Our fans grew quieter. The Spurs supporters, enjoying their day in the sun, jeered our strikers whenever they were on the ball.

In front of me, the shoulders of the manager seemed to sag with each passing minute. As the half-time whistle blew, he jumped up from his seat and walked quickly down the tunnel like a man with a train to catch.

He was waiting for us in the changing room, standing in silence at one end of the team. He waited for the lads to get a cup of tea, then began to speak.

It was a five-minute talk. He showed us where our weaknesses were and, just as importantly, where Spurs were looking vulnerable. He wasn't angry. He was determined, confident even. I looked around at the faces of the players who, a couple of minutes ago, had seemed tired and frustrated. There was a new look on their faces. They believed in themselves again.

As they filed out for the second half, the manager dropped back to walk beside me.

'Get warmed up, Geronimo,' he murmured. 'You're on in ten minutes.'

Unless we scored. He didn't have to say that. I knew football well enough to know that you don't change a strike force that has begun to score goals.

As the second half started, I jogged up and down the touchline, vaguely aware of a tremor of excitement in the stands behind me.

Lazlo. It was like a whisper, getting louder. Lazlo. Here he comes. Lazlo's coming on.

I glanced at the game and, for the first time in my life, I prayed that the City wouldn't score.

By the time I had returned to my seat, it was clear that Dodd was tiring, losing confidence – we could see that, and so could the Spurs defence. They were winding him up, expecting him to crack at any moment. After five minutes he lost the ball to the Spurs left back and, in a wild attempt to retrieve the situation, lunged at the player, catching his ankle and earning himself a yellow card.

Briefly Steve Malcolm buried his face in his hands, then he glanced over his shoulder. From our fans behind the Spurs goalmouth came a new sound.

*Clap clap. Clap-clap-clap. Clap-clap-clap-clap. Lazlo.*

At first, it was a quiet, restrained sound – more a question, a wondering aloud, than anything else. Then it got louder.

*Clap clap. Clap-clap-clap. Clap-clap-clap-clap-LAZLO!*

Soon the stand on the far side had joined in.

Steve Malcolm looked at his watch, then turned to me. 'All right, Geronimo.' He jerked his head. 'Get stripped off.'

I stood. The fans cheered. Lazlo was about to make his entrance.

The ball went out of play, and Joe Smith held the number 9 above his head. Georgie Dodd glanced across. At first, he seemed not to believe that he was being substituted. Then he jogged slowly towards where we stood. The linesman checked my studs.

Dodd shook my hand, looked into my eyes with undisguised hatred, and invited me to go and break my leg.

His problem, not mine. I sprinted on to the pitch to take up my position up front beside Kevin Miller.

Soon I was in the middle of a nightmare. Running for a ball that had come loose, I bundled clumsily into an opposing player, giving away a free kick.

Seconds later, I jumped for the ball and took it square on the side of the neck.

Unable to believe their luck, the Spurs fans began to cheer me mockingly every time I was near the ball. I glanced up towards the wall of City fans behind the Spurs goal. They were silent now, embarrassed by their new player.

'Relax, kid.' The voice of Budgie Burton came from behind. 'Play your normal game. You're trying too hard.'

Maybe he was right. I had been running and jumping like Stanley Peterson – pushing and straining. I had been like someone used to riding a pushbike who's suddenly behind the wheel of a Ferrari. I had to think like a champion, feel like a champion. I had to be Lazlo in my head as well as my body.

City were playing the ball out of defence. Whitcroft sent a diagonal ball to Budgie who hesitated, then threaded it through to me.

Laughter and jeers from the Spurs fans. Confident that I was going nowhere, the Spurs back four held back, waiting for me to foul up yet again.

Mistake.

The ball at my feet, I approached Baker. I dummied, pushed the ball to the byline and sprinted, beating him to it by an easy yard. I pulled back, dribbling into the box, skipping over another diving tackle, somehow instinctively aware that Fraser was arriving at the far post at about a hundred miles an hour.

The chip was perfect – no backlift, a hard, downward stubbing movement of the foot. The ball soared beyond the groping hands of the keeper. Five yards out, Fraser launched himself through the air – a brave diving header. It was there.

Pandemonium. A deafening roar from the crowd. Several of the team fell on to Fraser who was still lying on the ground. When he had shaken them off, he jogged over to me, slapped my hand.

I nodded, then glanced up at the clock. Ten minutes left. But we needed more to help our goal difference.

Like a real professional, Budgie had grabbed the ball and placed it on the centre spot. I sprinted back to take my place.

When I was Stanley Peterson, time would pass fast or slow during a game, depending on whether City were winning.

But now, for Lazlo, everything moved in a strange, dreamlike state. I was beyond time, above it. Looking around me, I could see the pattern of red-and-white City shirts as clearly as I if I were looking down on the game from high above the stadium.

Spurs? They were just desperate, scurrying shadows.

I moved forward, jogging. Richards, their central defender, was in possession. Ten yards in front of him, I put in a sudden spurt. Surprised by my speed, he unloaded the ball hurriedly, letting it fall to a City player, Darren Stringer, on the left.

Stringer. Burton. Into the penalty area. There were four City men in the box. I held back. Burton crossed the ball but the defender Gibson got a head to it. The ball soared away from the defence, over the head of Georgie Dodd, out of the area.

To Lazlo.

Nothing could stop me. As if I were alone, back in the corner of the playground, I chested the ball up. It hung in the air and, for that second, it seemed as if the entire stadium was holding its breath. It began to fall.

I pulled back my favourite left foot, glanced up at the target – and let fly.

It was as if all the strength and will in my body was being channelled through that foot, as if something superhuman was making contact with the ball. The result wasn't really a kick at all. It was a detonation, a controlled explosion of power. A force of nature.

I looked up. The ball was in the back of the net. The Spurs keeper hadn't moved.

A split second later, the crowd let out its breath in a great roar of astonishment and relief. The City players were running towards me.

I turned back to the halfway line. I wasn't interested in their congratulations. We needed another goal.

As Spurs kicked off once more, I felt for the first

time the agony of tension in the stadium, the clock ticking towards the moment when, if we didn't score, all our efforts might have been in vain. I became aware of the heart-stopping, choking panic of my team-mates who, so many times that season, had lost concentration in those last minutes. It wasn't the desire to win that was in their blood now – it was the fear of losing. And fear wins nothing.

Above all, I felt the new determination of the Spurs players. They were playing for pride now and they knew what they had to do. Stop Lazlo.

Even while Gibson kept possession for them, Baker and Richards shadowed me. Normally, a team can take advantage of two opposition players taking themselves out of the game, but there was a sort of panic in the way the City team were playing now.

If we were going to get something out of this game, it was down to me to do it.

There was a minute of normal time left. Our right back Billy Dean had gained possession. 'Bring it,' I muttered. 'Pass it round.'

But the crowd were screaming now. Instinctively Dean hoofed the ball in my direction. Too far. I pretended to scream angrily at the bad pass. Then, as my two markers relaxed for a fatal second, I swerved away from them in pursuit of the ball.

I was two yards up on both of them as the ball soared into the area. The wind whistled past my ears. It was a race between me and the Spurs keeper. A one-horse race.

Two yards short of the ball, I caught sight of a shape approaching out of the corner of my eye. A Spurs player – and he was heading for the ball. I tried to skip the wild, lunging tackle but I was too late. There was an explosion of pain in my ankle and I seemed to take off into space.

Pain – agony like I'd never known before. Sobbing, heaving gasps that seemed to be coming from me. As if from a great distance, I saw the referee hold up a red card. I didn't see which Spurs player was being sent off. I didn't care. There were seconds to go. I had been robbed of a goal.

Harry Wheeler, the City physio, was spraying my ankle. 'Just a knock,' he was saying. It sounded like a prayer. 'You'll be all right, Lazza.'

Among the players gathered around me, I saw Budgie Burton, the ball under his arm. Suddenly, I realized what was happening. City had a penalty. And the man who was planning to take it had missed three times from the spot in the last two months. I looked more closely at our tall, fair-haired mid-fielder. I saw fear, I saw defeat in his eyes.

I tested the ankle. Wheeler's prayers had been answered. It was still a red-hot ball of pain but I could move it. Nothing was broken.

Polite applause as Lazlo stood up, jogged carefully. Silence as he approached the captain.

'Lazlo will take the penalty,' I said. I took the ball from Burton. He made a show of reluctance but I could feel the relief flooding from him.

I walked slowly towards the penalty spot, weighing the ball in my hand.

I put the ball on the spot. As I walked back a few paces, silence descended on the stadium. I took a deep breath. In that moment of pure tension, I seemed to hear, as if from another universe, a distant voice calling me.

'Stanley,' it was saying. 'Stanley Peterson.'

The whistle blew.

*Lazlo.* I said it out loud. 'Lazlo.'

I ran forward, seeing the ball fly into the right-hand corner, knowing where it would go, believing it, willing it.

And it did.

An explosion of sound marked the goal. I was surrounded by City players. I stood tall. The referee pointed to the halfway line. The air seemed to be cut by the City fans' newest chant.

'Lazlo! Lazlo! Lazlo!'

Kick-off. A minute, maybe ninety seconds. Spurs had had enough. We kept possession. I hadn't touched the ball again before the final whistle blew. We walked off to a standing ovation.

Dean, Stringer and Field ran down to the left end to salute the fans.

'Lazlo! Lazlo! Lazlo!'

I walked slowly towards the tunnel where Steve Malcolm stood smiling.

'I think they want you, son.' He nodded in the direction of the fans.

But already my mind was on getting home. 'In a minute, boss,' I said. I pointed to my feet. 'Change my boots.'

My ankle was hurting again now. Limping, I made my way to the dressing room.

A stud spanner lay on the kit table. Grabbing it, I locked myself in one of the toilets.

For a moment, I hesitated. Then I closed my eyes and turned the key. There was the electric jolt I remembered. When I came round, I found myself staring at the skinny legs of Stanley Peterson.

I took off the boots, put the stud back in my pocket, unlocked the door.

There were voices outside the dressing room. The door opened. Whitcroft and Field stumbled, laughing, sweating. They stopped when they saw me.

'What you doing here?' asked Dave Whitcroft.

'I must have taken a wrong turning.'

I smiled, then took out my programme. 'Could I have your autograph, please?'

It was a daze, a sort of thick fog which filled my brain, made my head and my eyes and my bones ache. There was a burning pain in my ankle. My fists were still clenched at my side, just as they had been after I had scored the penalty. Physically, I may have been Stanley again, but part of me was still Lazlo.

I was aware of people staring at me as I made my way back in football boots to the family stand and into the toilet where, to my relief, my trainers were still hidden. As I emerged, I saw Callan and Angie talking to a steward.

'There he is!' Callan pointed at me as I approached.

'What happened to you? You missed the best match ever,' said Angie.

The steward was looking at me oddly. 'You all right, son? You're very pale.'

'*Yesss!*' Even I was surprised by the roar of triumph that emerged from my throat. 'I mean, yes. Thank you.'

'Did you see that Lazlo?' Angie laughed. 'They put two men on him, they tried to break his leg – and he still won the match for us.'

'Yeah, and he looks such a skinny little runt,' said Callan.

'What?' I took a step towards him.

'At first when he came on I thought he was the mascot.'

My head throbbing, I pointed a warning finger. 'Don't ever *ever* talk like that about Lazlo again.'

Callan glanced uncertainly at Angie.

'Your friend takes his game a bit seriously, doesn't he?' the steward murmured.

But I had turned and was limping towards the exit.

'Stanley?' I heard Callan's voice behind me. 'What's got into you?'

# CHAPTER 10

## Sometimes you have to lie . . .

. . . to your mum. It happens, and there's nothing you can do about it.

Limping home, as I listened to Callan and Angie ranting and raving about Lazlo, I had calmed down enough to work out my alibi.

I had decided to try to get some autographs. I had sneaked around to the players' entrance. To get back to my seat I would have had to pass through the Spurs fans in my City kit. The stewards kept me there throughout the game. Bummer.

Trouble is, I've never been that good at lying. While the expert porky-teller keeps it simple, then quickly changes the the subject of conversation, I'm so eager to make it sound good that I keep on talking, building lie upon lie like a house of cards until it all collapses.

'The steward was really nice,' I said to Mum, after Callan and Angie had dropped me off. 'He told me all sorts of things about the team. I saw the dressing room.'

'How kind of him.' Mum sat at the kitchen table, stirring her tea. 'What was his name?'

'Name?'

'The steward.'

Panic. 'Stuart,' I said rather too quickly.

'Stuart. A steward called Stuart.'

'Yeah, funny that. He said all the other guys teased him about it. He was thinking of using his second name – Michael – but then he . . . decided not to.'

My mother was looking at me oddly.

'He had red hair,' I struggled on. 'Quite short.'

'Hm.' Mum can put more feeling into a 'Hm' than most people can manage in a sentence. This 'Hm' meant: I don't believe a word of this but I'm going to let you get away with it, just so long as you know you haven't fooled me for one second.

'What about your foot? You're limping.'

'Fell down some stairs,' I said, suddenly feeling tired. 'I sprained my ankle.'

She leant down and pulled up my tracksuit trousers. The bone of my left ankle was swollen and red. 'That's not a sprain. It's a knock.'

'Someone tripped over me when I was on the ground. Great big fat bloke.'

'Stuart?'

'Yes – I mean no. Stuart was quite kind. He . . .

told me he had lots of cats. He gave me a cup of coffee.'

'You don't like coffee.'

'Yeah, funny that. I suddenly seemed to like it. And it didn't have sugar in it. Maybe I was in shock.' I sighed, exhausted by all this crazy invention.

'What's going on, Stanley?' There was an odd look on my mother's face. Sort of disappointed and worried at the same time.

'Nothing.' I wished I could tell her what had happened but I couldn't. Not until after the Liverpool game. 'I think I'll have a lie-down. I'm exhausted.' Without another word, I turned and limped up the stairs.

I opened my football bag and took out the stud. It had been slightly worn down. I put it under my pillow, lay on the bed in my clothes. I closed my eyes and slept.

'Stan.' Someone was shaking me. 'Stanley.'

I opened my eyes. On the end of the bed sat Callan and Angie. I was in my pyjamas and the sun was shining through the window.

'What time is it?'

'Past ten,' said Callan.

'On Sunday,' said Angie. 'You've just beaten the world sleeping record. Your mum said you crashed out at six last night. She reckons the tension of the relegation battle's getting to you.'

'Maybe.' I sat up in bed.

'We thought you'd like to see the papers.' She picked up one of several newspapers that were on the bed, and read the headlines: '*Mystery striker to the rescue. Who is Lazza? Malcolm's secret signing sinks Spurs.*' She handed it to me.

There were pictures of Lazlo – mobbed by the City team after my first goal, striking the penalty, walking off the pitch, eyes fixed on the tunnel, at the end of the game.

We looked at the newspapers for a moment in silence. Normally the only times City gets in the news is when a bigger club is just about to buy one of our best players. Grabbing the headlines for the right reasons felt good.

'He reminds me of someone,' Callan said suddenly.

I looked more closely at the photographs. The eyes. The way he stood. The smile. There was no mistaking the resemblance to me.

'Doesn't look like anyone I can think of,' I said casually. 'What else do the papers say?'

'One of them says they've heard he might be too injured to play Liverpool,' said Angie.

That was a point. I moved my left ankle. It was sore but felt better than last night.

'He'll be OK,' I said. 'Young bones.'

'They all tried to interview him after the game but Steve Malcolm said he was very shy,' said Callan.

'Shy? The way he strutted about the pitch?' Angie laughed. 'I spoke to Pete from school last night. He

70

went to the game with Miss Tysoe. He says she's fallen in love with him.'

'Miss Tysoe and Lazlo.' Callan shook his head. 'I can't see it.'

'She said she almost felt as if they had met somewhere before.' Angie was flicking through one of the papers. 'She's well gone, apparently.' She glanced up, then narrowed her eyes. 'Why are you blushing, Stan?'

'I – I forgot to do my homework. You just reminded me.'

Angie and Callan looked at one another, then back at me. 'Homework?' said Callan. 'City have just beaten Spurs 3–0. They've found the striker of the season – and you're talking about homework?'

I shrugged. 'Sorry,' I said.

After Callan and Angie had gone, I lay in bed for a while. I still felt strange, with an odd tingling at the back of my head. I had the weirdest sensation that I was still in a dream. The memory of being Lazlo suddenly seemed more real than lying here on my bed, the newspapers on my lap.

And now what? Lazlo may have kept City's hopes alive for another game, the last match of the season, but was he going to be able to appear out of nowhere once more for the Liverpool game? How was Steve Malcolm going to explain the disappearance of his star player to the press? For a moment I wished Lazlo was somebody else, that he didn't depend on being me.

But that wasn't possible. I was Lazlo. Lazlo was me. If I wanted to save City, I was going to have to find a way round these problems.

And all the time, as the Stanley Peterson part of my brain thought with as much logic as the Stanley Peterson part of my brain has ever managed, Lazlo was there too, reliving yesterday's match, thinking of the next game, his mind full of football, only football.

I got up, put the stud in my pocket and made my way along the corridor. From behind the half-closed door of my mum's office, I could hear the familiar hums and clicks of the computer.

I pushed the door. Still in her dressing gown, Mum was plugged into the machine, electronic hairnet in place, staring at the screen like a zombie on a bad-hair day. The green car wasn't moving, wasn't changing colour.

'Traffic jam?' I said quietly.

Mum started slightly, then turned to me.

'I can't get it to do anything,' she said, taking off the headband. 'For the last two days, it seems to have gone on strike.'

'Yeah?' I winced to myself. 'Maybe you're not thinking hard enough.'

'It's probably just me.' She yawned wearily. 'There's a theory that powering the computer with your synapses actually weakens you – destroys your brain cells.'

I stared at her, my mind turning over the full horror of what she was saying.

'Of course, we're losing brain cells all the time, so small acts of computer-generated activity wouldn't be too much of a problem. But if we get to major cybertelekinesis – generating important changes with our minds – nobody really knows what the effects might be.' She laughed. 'It's probably why I crash out at the end of the day.' She turned to look at me.

'Scary,' I said quietly.

She smiled. 'Don't worry, love. The minor stuff I'm doing won't do any harm.'

'Need some breakfast,' I muttered. In a daze, I wandered out of the room and downstairs.

The destruction of brain cells. Major cyberteleki-nesis. I stood in the kitchen, staring out of the window at the street outside. Cybertelekinesis didn't get much more major than creating a real-life football superhero.

I tapped the side of my head, hoping to revive the braincells which right now were probably pegging out in their thousands. Maybe I should give them a test. *Nine nines.* I couldn't remember! My mind was a blank! *63?* That didn't sound right. *72?* By tomorrow the five times table would have gone. Eventually two twos would be beyond me.

Maybe this was the price I was going to pay for saving the City. They'd be in the Premier League but I'd be bumping into walls and forgetting my own name. They'd probably give me a VIP seat in the Executive box, where I'd sit, all blank-eyed and vacant, even when we scored a goal. Kids would point at me.

'Who's that, Dad?'

'That's Stanley Peterson, son. He gave his brains for the City.'

'Cor.'

*81!* Suddenly it was there. Hang on in there, brain cells.

# CHAPTER 11

## 'So much for Superman . . .'

. . . Matthew Turner slammed a copy of the *Daily Star* on the desk in front of me as, two days later, I sat waiting for the first lesson of the day. Matthew used to be a City fan until he discovered that he knew someone whose grandfather once lived quite near Manchester, which was a good enough reason for him to start supporting Manchester United. There was nothing that gave him greater pleasure than bringing bad news about the team he used to support.

'What are you on about?' I looked down at the newspaper in front of me. Its front page headline read: *LAZZA SCORES AGAIN! Football star in shock nightclub scenes.*

Trying to seem casual, I read through the report.

*The mystery of football's disappearing superstar was*

*solved last night when City striker Lazlo was spotted in the early hours of Monday morning at a West End nightclub — drunk, foul-mouthed and out of control. The wayward star astonished clubbers and staff, DRINKING from bottles of champagne, KISSING the two girls he was with and ABUSING our photographer. City manager Steve Malcolm, who had appealed to Lazlo to contact him, now seems certain to come under pressure to sack his wayward star. Full story and pictures on pages 3, 4 and 5.*

My heart beating, I opened the paper. With the story on the inside pages, there were four photographs — one of a man dancing very closely to a woman in the darkness of a club, another of him swigging at a bottle, another of him slumped, eyes half closed, between two girls, and the last of him being driven away in a large back limousine.

It was this last shot that was the clearest. The man had opened the window and was making an angry gesture at the photographer.

'That's not him,' I said quietly. 'It's a fake.'

'Looks like him to me,' said Matthew.

Miss Tysoe wandered up behind us and stared at the paper with a fine show of casualness. 'I don't believe it,' she murmured.

'Lazlo's done a runner.' Matthew chuckled nastily. 'He won't be playing for your lot again. Says so.'

I read the article more closely. Most of what had

been written was guesswork and fantasy – Lazlo was unhappy in Britain, Lazlo had a drink problem, Lazlo had left a wife and three children in his home country of Latvia – but the quotes from Steve Malcolm seemed genuine enough.

'No one player is bigger than this club,' the City manager had told the *Star*. 'Whatever this lad's problems, we can't have him running around town bringing the good name of City Football Club into disrepute. If he fails to report for training tomorrow, I shall not be including him in my plans for the Liverpool game.'

'I wonder how they got the story,' said Miss Tysoe.

'Martin Sturgess,' I said. 'He's the only player quoted in the paper. And he hates Lazlo.'

'How come you know so much?' sneered Matthew.

'I just do.' I looked more closely at the pictures. The man at the club and in the car was dark like Lazlo; he had Lazlo's hair and sleepy eyes. But it wasn't Lazlo. My brain cells may have been fading but I think I would have remembered something like that.

Miss Tysoe had walked to the front of the class. She rapped her desk with her knuckle and gradually silence descended on the classroom. 'Morning, everyone,' she said, and smiled palely.

The lesson passed quickly. Ever since I had been Lazlo, I had found it easier to work. The game against Liverpool was always there, somewhere at the back of my brain, but meanwhile I could concentrate on Stanley Peterson's work. My life was divided, but neat. I knew where I was going.

'Angie, how could someone get to meet Steve Malcolm?'

It was break-time and I had been thinking about the Lazlo problem. If anyone could help me it was Angie.

'He gets to his office at the City ground soon after eight o'clock and does his correspondence. By ten, he will have left for the training ground where he spends the rest of the morning. One-thirty to two-thirty, it's back to the office and the afternoon's spent seeing people, in meetings, watching the reserves.'

'Hm.' I nodded thoughtfully. It wasn't even worth asking Angie how she knew all these things – where City was concerned, she was a walking encyclopedia.

'What about away from the stadium?' I asked.

'He lives in the suburbs, about ten minutes from the ground.' I held my breath. She couldn't know his address, could she?

'23 Broadhurst Avenue.'

She could. 'Cheers, Ange,' I said.

'What's it for?' she asked.

'I'm doing a composition for Miss Tysoe. It's called "The day I met my hero".'

'Yeah?' There was no fooling Angie. She was suspicious. 'Maybe you should meet Lazlo instead.'

'Maybe.' I wandered off. When I glanced back, Angie was still watching me.

Mum was in a bad mood when I got home – I could tell by the quiet, angry way she was ironing things in the bedroom. When something goes wrong in her private life, Mum always turns to the ironing board.

'What's up?' I asked.

'Nothing.'

. . . Two, three, four. Mum can keep her annoyance to herself for ten seconds maximum. Eight, nine—

'Oh by the way, the Dweeble rang for you today. He was in one one of his Concerned Dad moods.'

'Ah, right. What did he say?'

'He says he's got good tickets for the Liverpool match.'

Oh great. As if life wasn't complicated enough. 'I'm not sure,' I said. 'I promised Callan and Angie I'd go with them.'

'You tell him, then.' Mum leant forward, grinding the iron downwards. 'Otherwise he'll think it was me who tried to put you off.'

'OK.'

'On the other hand, maybe you ought to see him,' she said. 'After all, it is the last match of the season and the Dweeble goes into hibernation if there's no football.'

'That's true.' I glanced at my watch. I had a

football manager to track down. 'I'm just going round to Callan's house.'

'Don't be late.' Mum's voice still had an anti-Dweeble tremor in it.

'I won't.' I hesitated at the door. 'Mum, I think you've done that shirt now.'

She looked up and narrowed her eyes. 'Sometimes you remind me so much of your father.'

'Thanks, Mum.'

I got out of the house before the missiles started flying.

# CHAPTER 12

## Steve Malcolm was famous . . .

. . . for liking his privacy. Other managers might parade their wives in the executive box at the ground, chat about their kids, pose with the family for photographs in magazines, but not Steve. 'That's personal,' he would tell any journalist who dared to ask about his life away from the City Stadium.

So I expected to find a big wall or electric fence patrolled by Dobermanns when I arrived at the address Angie had given me. Instead, I found a house like all the others in the avenue – large, modern, with a lawn between the house and the road that ran past it. In the drive was parked a Jaguar XL which, thanks to Angie, I knew belonged to Steve Malcolm.

Ten, fifteen times, I passed the gate, plucking up courage to ring the bell. Apart from the distant hum of traffic and the sound of someone playing the piano nearby, all was silence. I was just about to give up when the front door to number 23 opened. There, in the neat casual clothes for which he was well known, stood the manager of City Football Club.

'What's your game?' he said in a voice that was somehow different from the one I had heard on a thousand interviews.

'Sorry to bother you, boss – I mean, Mr Malcolm. But I need to talk to you.'

'Not now, son.' He turned away.

'It's really important.' The door was closing. 'It's about Lazlo.'

That stopped him.

'Listen, son, I'm very busy, I've had a tough week, I haven't seen my wife and children all day.' He hesitated. 'What about Lazlo, anyway?'

'I know where he is.'

'Yeah? How come you know Lazlo?'

'I'm . . . kind of related to him.'

'When did you last see him?'

Tricky one. 'I see him quite often – every day, in fact. He wanted me to give you a message.'

'I get it. You're doing a little spying job for the press, aren't you?' He shook his head. 'Those guys will try anything.'

'I'll prove it.' I called out, desperate to stop him closing the door in my face again. 'In the dressing room before the game, you dropped Martin Sturgess from the subs' bench. You told Lazlo to fit in behind the front two. You called me – I mean, him – Geronimo.'

The manager frowned. 'How did you know that?'

'Lazlo told me.'

He opened the door. Muttering 'Five minutes is your limit', he nodded for me to follow.

I was shown into a room with big windows and paintings on the wall and immaculate seats and tables, not a speck of dust anywhere.

'Stay in here.' For the first time, I realized how different Steve Malcolm was from the helpful, friendly character he seemed to be when interviewed. 'And don't touch anything.'

Nervously, I sat on a red, high-backed chair which looked as if it had just arrived from the shop that day.

The door opened. A dark, pretty woman I recognized as Mrs Malcolm stared at me.

'Steve ees saying goodnight to the keeds,' she said in a heavy foreign accent. 'He'll be with you in a minute.'

'Yeah, fine. Back of the net.'

She looked at me for a moment. 'Blinkin' football,' she said suddenly. 'Wasta time, innit.'

I shrugged and she had gone.

Football a waste of time? In the house of Steve Malcolm? I looked around me. On the mantelpiece were a couple of team photographs, and a corner cupboard nearby was full of trophies but the room seemed to suggest a man for whom football was just a job, a way of earning a living.

'Right.' The man himself walked in briskly. Saying goodnight to his children didn't seem to have improved his mood. 'What's all this about then?' He sat down in the chair opposite me and drummed the fingers of his right hand impatiently on the arm.

'Lazlo says he's sorry for what has happened and that—'

'Hang on, hang on.' Steve Malcolm held up a hand. 'Don't they have telephones where this bloke comes from? If he's got to get messages to me, what's he doing using some kid?'

'It's difficult to explain.' I was beginning to regret coming here.

'Try me,' he said.

'Lazlo's background's a bit . . . complicated. He had things to sort out – problems.'

The manager gave a humourless laugh. 'Problems he had to sort out with the help of a few bottles of champagne and some girls at a club.'

'That wasn't him,' I said quickly. 'The journalists made it all up. He's never been in a club in his life.'

'Never? Why not?'

'They wouldn't let him in. He's too . . . famous. He's very well known where he comes from.'

'What's he got to say for himself, then?'

'What he asked me to tell you is . . .' I braced myself for the manager's reaction. 'He can't make tomorrow's practice.'

'What d'you mean, "can't"?' Steve Malcolm's voice was dangerously quiet. 'Give me one reason why a City Football Club player can't attend training.'

'He's still a bit injured.'

'All the more reason to be there. The club physio could work on him.'

What could I say? That he couldn't get off school? That he didn't know how to get to the training ground? That he was afraid of losing brain cells?

'He'll be available for the Liverpool game,' I said. 'He'll be there, I promise.'

'This is ridiculous.' The manager stood up.

With amazing coolness, I managed to stay in my seat. A thought had occurred to me. 'I know that everyone says you should discipline Lazlo—'

'Everyone?' Steve Malcolm's eyes flashed angrily. 'Who's everyone?'

'Journalists. Some of the players. Other managers.'

'They don't manage City. I do. I'll make my own decisions about discipline, Lazlo and anything else that concerns City Football Club.'

'Of course, Mr Malcolm.' I managed to suppress a smile and stood up. 'Lazlo says sorry and, if you want him, he'll be there on Saturday.'

For the first time, the manager seemed unsure of himself. When he spoke, it was in a friendlier voice than he had used before. 'Tell him that, if he's at the City stadium by ten on Saturday morning – not one minute later – and, if he passes a fitness test, I might – *might* – consider him for the team.'

'Yes, Mr Malcolm.'

'And tell him to ignore what he reads in the papers. I'll include him in the squad of fifteen to be considered for Saturday. Tell him . . .' He hesitated and, for that moment, I could see the pressure and stress that he was feeling. 'Tell him I'm not doing it for him but for the club. This is the last time.'

'I think he knows that.'

He held the door open. As I passed him, he laid a hand on my shoulder. 'What is this?' he asked. 'What exactly's going on here?'

I smiled. 'I can't tell you,' I said. 'Maybe Lazlo will explain on Saturday.'

'Steve?' Mrs Malcolm stood at the top of the stairs. 'Is that leetle fan gone now?'

'He's going.' To my surprise, Steve Malcolm held out a hand. I shook it. 'This discussion didn't happen. Understand?'

'What discussion?'

'Good lad.' He held open the front door. 'What was your name again?'

'Doesn't matter,' I said. 'It's Lazlo that matters.'

The manager nodded. 'This is true,' he murmured. 'This is true.'

# CHAPTER 13

## I never ate sweets now . . .

. . . and hardly ever kicked a tennis ball about in the playground. When Callan asked me about this, I told him I didn't want to get injured. He thought I was joking. I didn't talk much, not at school, not at home. I was careful about my diet. With every second, I felt more Lazlo, less Stanley.

'Stanley, you do realize you're becoming extremely weird, don't you?'

It was Thursday and Angie was walking beside me on our way home after school.

'Weird? Angie Weston calling me weird. I've heard it all now.'

'In lessons, you don't want to hear about City. You complain that school dinners are low in polyunsaturated whatsits when you've never even thought about food before. And, look at you – you're even walking differently. Like some sort of wannabe athlete or something.'

'Get over it, Angie.'

'There you go. You never would have said something like that before. Stanley Peterson, Mr Tough Guy? I don't think so.'

'I need your help,' I said.

'What kind of help?'

'Come and have tea and I'll tell you.'

Of course, it was Lazlo who needed the help. After seeing Steve Malcolm, I had made the biggest decision of my life. I'd risk my brain cells and be Lazlo just once more.

But, if Lazlo was playing Liverpool, he needed to know a bit more about the opposition. The truth was that I had always been so obsessed by City that I had never paid much attention to other teams. That was where Angie came in – she didn't know it, but she was just about to brief one of the greatest footballers who had ever trod the sacred turf of the City Stadium.

Me.

'Hi, kids.' When we got home, Mum was in the kitchen, in front of the cooker, preparing supper with the help of a cookbook.

Eh?

'What are you doing, Mum?'

'Hi, darling. Hi, Angie.'

She looked up, then returned to the cookbook in

front of her. 'Dice the carrots, then add a zest of lemon.'

'Mum, please, don't.'

'Don't what?'

'Try to behave like a mother. It gives me the creeps.'

'I am a mother. I've got you steak and spinach, like you asked. Now I'm preparing a little rocket salad.'

I shook my head. Mum in the kitchen with a cookbook. Next thing, she'd be wanting to read to me or teach me the rules of chess or take me to the theatre.

'I just need to discuss something with Angie,' I said.

'Don't be too long. We've got a doctor's appointment at half past five.'

'Eh?'

'Just a check-up.' Mum started chopping up a carrot in a very inexpert way. 'And please don't say "Eh?" like that.'

'But . . . a check-up. Why?'

My mother glanced at Angie. 'I'll tell you on the way.'


Angie's not exactly the most inquisitive person in the world. She takes everything as it comes. Probably, if I'd told her that, thanks to the biggest breakthrough in the history of computers, I could cybertelekinetically turn into the best striker in the league and save

City from relegation, her only worry would be that there were no statistics for Lazlo in her little notebook.

Because, for Angie, if something didn't have facts and figures, it didn't exist.

But I wasn't going to risk telling her about Lazlo. Somehow, instinctively, I sensed that part of his power lay in the secret of his existence.

'I was just thinking,' I said as we sat on the bed in my room. 'If I knew everything that mattered about Liverpool, I could be a better fan on Saturday.'

'So what d'you want to know?' said Angie, buying this lame excuse as if it was the most natural thing in the world. She opened her notebook.

'How much do we need to win by to stay in the Premier League?'

'Right, two teams are already down. The third relegation spot is between us, Coventry and West Ham. They've both got quite tough games.'

'But not as tough as ours.'

She nodded. 'They're against Aston Villa and Blackburn. Both of those teams are on a winning streak but they've got nothing to play for. They're in Europe next season whatever happens. Villa are in the Cup Final and so their minds might be on that. They might even rest a couple of players.'

'While Liverpool could win the championship?'

'Theoretically. They're a point behind Newcastle – but Newcastle are away to Wimbledon who have beaten them a surprising four times in the last three seasons. If you take goal difference into account—'

'Just tell me the worst that can happen, Angie.'

'If Coventry and the Hammers both win on Saturday, we have to beat Liverpool.'

'By how many goals?'

'Doesn't matter. Our goal difference is good. The other two would have to score more than five goals to overtake us.'

'All we have to do is beat Liverpool.'

'Who are unbeaten in ten games, have no injury problems and are firm favourites to win the championship.' She allowed herself a smile. 'Easy, right?'

It was my turn to smile. 'Tell me about their defence.'

Angie turned a page in her notebook. 'Pechnik's the best keeper in the league,' she said. 'He's let in fewer goals this season than any other keeper and has saved five out of seven penalties this year. He's a bit of a crazy character – comes out of his area a lot, takes a few chances, but almost always gets away with them. Two weeks ago, he came up for a Liverpool corner in the last minute of the game and scored.'

'I'm not interested in their attack.' Maybe I spoke more sharply than I intended because Angie pursed her lips disapprovingly.

'Their most reliable central defender is the England international, Alan Holdsworth. Very tough, always in the right place, never concedes a penalty, great in the air.'

'But slow.'

'He's lost a yard of pace over the last couple of seasons but he's quicker than he looks. They'll probably play Steve Charles beside him. Now he is fast. He may be a bit small for a defender but he can outjump most strikers. If there's a danger man in the opposition, Charles will be the one to do the marking job. He's like a limpet. He's had a few yellow cards this season but he's a cool customer.'

'Full backs?'

'On the left is Bjornson, the Swedish international. Quick, goes forward a lot but rarely gets caught out of position. On the right is the Under-21 international Gary Fenton. According to the papers, he's a bit raw and inexperienced but he's been in the team all year. If they're not winning by the last ten minutes, he's the one to come off to make way for an extra striker. And in midfield—'

'Defensive midfield.'

'Yeah, thank you, Stanley, defensive midfield.' Angie frowned as she looked at her notes. I felt guilty for being rude to her but I needed this information. In fact, right now it seemed more important to me than any friendship.

'They play the Irish international Brian O'Reilly in front of the back four. You know about him – he's a bit of a bruiser and he's got a bad temper on him. He's been sent off nine times in his career but all the commentators say he's the backbone of the team. He's broken his right leg and missed a couple of games two seasons ago with a cracked knuckle.'

I winced. 'Yeah, I remember. Someone said something to him in a nightclub.'

'Somehow I don't think Dodd and Miller will be tangling with him.'

There was a knock at the door. 'Time to go, Stanley.'

'I don't believe this,' I muttered. 'Why on earth would I need a check-up?'

'Search me,' said Angie, standing up. She put her notebook in the pocket of her jeans. 'I'll see you, Stan,' she said, making for the door. 'I don't know what's got into you these days. You've changed, somehow.'

Changed? If only she knew.

# CHAPTER 14

## Fat, scruffy, short of breath . . .

. . . and friendly, Dr Ian Barber was the kind of doctor they say doesn't really exist any more. Behind the paper-strewn desk, he looked at the world over his little glasses in a way that suggested that nothing anyone said in his surgery could surprise or shock him. I had been seeing him all my life and sometimes he seemed more of a family adviser than a doctor. Ever since Dad had left home, my mother had been taking me to the surgery for regular check-ups even if I was completely healthy. Dr Barber didn't seem to mind. He just booked us into his last appointment and chatted away as if he had all the time in the world.

Once or twice, I had caught him looking at Mum over those little specs and I wondered whether there was a bit more than doctorly interest in his attitude to her but, when I once mentioned it to Mum, she had seemed genuinely surprised.

'So how's it's all going?' Dr Barber gave her a warm, twinkly smile as we entered his surgery.

Mum frowned and, for one horrible moment, I thought she was going to confide in him about the brain cell problem. 'It's been a bad week,' she said. 'But I'll bounce back.'

A misty smile came over the doctor's face as if, for just a moment, he was imagining Mum bouncing back. Then he turned to me.

'So are we going to survive?'

'Sorry?'

'City. I always thought you were a City fan.'

'I am.' I had forgotten that the doctor liked a little fan-to-fan talk with me.

'Shame about this Lazlo fellow disappearing. He sounded like mustard.'

I shrugged modestly. 'He was OK,' I said.

'No football, please,' warned my mother in a tragic voice. 'Otherwise I really will be ill.'

'So.' The doctor leant back in his chair and rested both hands on his paunch. 'What's the story?'

'I'm a bit worried about Stanley.' Mum gave me an apologetic little smile. 'He's suddenly become obsessed with eating the right food. He seems to be concentrating on his work at school in a way he's never done before. He used to be a pain at bedtimes. Now he positively runs upstairs to bed. Falls asleep within seconds. He hardly talks at all. It's as if he's in a sort of trance. Yesterday, I caught him running up the stairs, three steps at a time. Again and again.'

'Just keeping fit,' I muttered.

'So you're eating well, getting lots of sleep and doing your school work.' Dr Barber smiled at me. 'Some mothers are never satisfied, are they?'

Mum ignored the joke. 'I spoke to his teacher and she said she'd noticed a difference, too. In the playground, he's always by himself – sitting, jogging, doing exercises. I don't know – it's just not Stanley somehow. He seems like a stranger.'

'Take your shirt off, Stan.'

I unbuttoned my shirt and took it off. I felt his cold hand on my shoulder. As he put his stethoscope on my back and then my heart, he chatted away casually to me as if we were alone.

'Anything on your mind, is there, Stanley?'

'Not really.'

'What about City? You must be a bit worried about them.'

'They're going to be all right.'

'And your dad? Have you seen him recently?'

I sighed. Mum and Dr Barber have got this idea that Dad's leaving home was this big crisis for me. 'Not for a while. He may be coming to the match on Saturday.'

'Oh aye, they'll all be coming along on Saturday – the fair-weather fans.'

'It's not exactly fair weather, trying to beat

relegation,' I said more loudly than I had intended. 'It's not Dad's fault that he can't get to all the games.'

'Hm.' The doctor nodded, as if my anger had confirmed his worst suspicions. 'I guess you miss him, eh?'

I shrugged. 'Sometimes.'

The doctor put the stethoscope on my chest. 'Maybe you both miss him.'

I glanced at Mum. To my surprise, she was blushing.

'I've been a bit preoccupied recently,' she said. 'My research is at a very exciting stage. I'm afraid I haven't been a very good mother.'

'You have,' I protested. 'I like it when you're working.'

Dr Barber was frowning. 'This heartbeat.' He shook his head, then looked at his notes. 'It's quite extraordinarily slow.'

'Is that bad?' I asked.

'Bad? No, it's good. You have the heartbeat of a top athlete. I can't understand why it's slowed down since your last check-up.'

'Maybe I'm just very fit.'

The doctor smiled. 'You're certainly fit, Stanley. I think I'll just take some blood to check your iron level.'

I groaned. 'Not an injection.'

'A small one. We'll patch you up with Popeye.'

I groaned, laughing. Ever since I had been coming to the surgery, Dr Barber had used jokey sticking plaster showing Popeye's face. Even now, when I was old enough not to cry at the thought of an injection, he used to produce his Popeye plaster from the top drawer of his desk as if I was still three and this was the biggest treat imaginable.

'You're never too old for Popeye.' The doctor dabbed at my right arm with cotton wool. 'Eh, Mrs Peterson?' He was giving her the full twinkle treatment again.

Mum smiled, then looked away. 'Very true, doctor,' she said.

# CHAPTER 15

## Thump thump thump . . .

. . . That famous slow heartbeat of mine drives me through the last day before the match. Nothing in everyday life seems real to me now. I'm going through the motions, preparing, storing energy. I'm ready. Lazlo is ready.

'I'm worried about what Dr Barber said.' Breakfast. Mum's looking at me as I eat my high-protein, low-sugar breakfast. 'Why should your heartbeat be so slow?'

'There's nothing to worry about.'

'It's not right.'

'I'm fine, Mum.'

Thump. Thump. Thump. Callan joins me on the way to school.

'Lazlo's in the squad. Says in the paper.'

'I know.'

99

'Aren't you excited or anything?'

'Cal, I've got to do something tomorrow morning. I'll pick up my ticket tonight and meet you at the ground, right?'

'Yeah, cool. You all right, Stan? You seem a bit . . . out of it today.'

'I'm fine. Back of the net, man.'

Thump. Thump. Thump. At school, every conversation I hear seems to be about the match tomorrow. Or maybe it's just that, for me, nothing matters, nothing exists, except the match. There's a hollow at the pit of my stomach. I want to be out there. On the pitch. Unbeatable.

I'm in the playground. It's breaktime. I close my eyes. The shouting and screaming around me have become a mighty wall of sound.

*City! City! City! City!*

Once I was part of that sound. Now it's behind me, lifting me. Pushing me. Into battle. I feel like a warrior.

*City! City! City! City!*

Someone's shaking my shoulder. I open my eyes. Miss Tysoe.

'Stanley? Are you all right? You seemed to be having some kind of fit.' She runs a hand across my forehead. 'Cold sweat,' she says. 'You're sickening for something.'

'I'm fine, miss.'

She looks doubtful, then smiles. 'The match is getting to me too,' she says.

Thump. Thump. Thump. We're in the queue for dinner. Accidentally on purpose Matthew Turner jogs Lizzie Dobbs so that she spills some soup down the back of my jeans.

Matthew laughs. 'Stanley's cacked himself. He must be thinking of his team playing Liverpool tomorrow.'

I feel a surge of rage within me. I put down my plate. Nobody does that to Lazlo.

I clench my fists. Matthew's squaring up to me. The boys are shouting us on. The dinner lady's laughing.

I step forward. Take a deep breath. Then stop. Mustn't get injured. Mustn't risk losing the stud. I smile at Matthew, then turn away.

'Got any chicken for Stanley?' Matthew taunts me as I take my dinner. 'Cluck cluck. Special meal for City fans.'

I walk away. The dinner lady tells Matthew he should be ashamed of himself but there's admiration in her voice.

Thump. Thump. Thump. On my way home, alone, I call in at Angie's house to pick up my ticket. After yesterday, she's still acting funny towards me. She avoids my eyes, almost as if she's afraid of what I've become.

I say, 'I'll see you at the ground then.'

'Fine. Back of the net.'

'And if I'm not there, it'll mean I've met up with my dad.'

She looks shocked, disappointed. 'You're not going to watch this match with us?'

'It's difficult. You know, families.'

'This is City, Stan. They're facing relegation. They need us.'

Stanley feels bad about Angie. But Lazlo has other things on his mind. 'I have to go, Ange.'

Thump. Thump. Thump. Mum has prepared a pasta supper. I eat it in silence. I turn down the chocolate mousse. She's had another bad day playing magic cars on the computer.

'Maybe brainwaves get weaker over time.' She's almost talking to herself. 'If the current generated by the alpha waves in the left lobe is essentially caused by a cognitive force field – what we call "will-power" – then it's only natural that it should start strong, then fade quite quickly.'

'Eh?' Suddenly I'm paying attention.

'Don't talk with your mouth full. And don't say "Eh?" You're not at a football match now.'

'The current gets weaker?'

'As scientists, we're dealing with neurons and cybernetic capacity. But, in the end, it comes down to human nature. At first, we want something really strongly, but pretty quickly our brains are taking in other things. The will fades like memory – it isn't as strong as it was. The flood of neurons generated by the synapses has got to slow down to a trickle quite quickly. That's why I can't move the car any more. However much I want it to be, the will isn't there.'

She sees me staring at her, no longer eating.

'Eat up, Stanley. I can't believe you're that fascinated in my work.'

I return to my pasta, my mind racing. It's the one thing I haven't planned for. Everything's in place for the return of Lazlo. But maybe my brainpower won't be strong enough. Mum's words echo in my head. *However much I want it to be, the will isn't there.*

Thump. Thump. Thump. The telephone rings after supper. Mum picks up the receiver. From her face, I can tell who it is. She holds out the telephone as if it's a rotten fish. 'Dweeble alert,' she says. I take the call in her bedroom upstairs.

'Hi, Dad.'

'Hullo, son. Sorry I've been a bit ... busy recently.'

'That's all right. I've been busy too.'

'Ready for the big one?'

'Yeah.'

'Any chance of seeing you at the game?'

Not in the way you think, Dad. 'I'm going with Callan and Angie.'

'Oh, right. I'd see you afterwards but I'm staying with a friend this weekend, so it's a bit difficult.'

'Not to worry. A new friend?'

'Yeah.' An embarrassed laugh. 'You'd like her.'

'What happened to Stephanie?' That was his last new friend.

'Didn't work out. She supports Chelsea. Say no more.'

'Yeah, right. Say no more.'

'I'll call you next week, then.'

Sure you will. 'Yeah.'

'Fingers crossed for tomorrow, eh?'

'Yeah.' Pause. 'Wish me luck, Dad.'

'Eh? For what?'

'Just wish me luck.'

'All right. Good luck, son.'

'Thanks, Dad. Bye.'

'Bye, Stan.'

Thump. Thump. Thump.

'Are you all right, Stanley?' I'm still on the bed upstairs. Mum puts her arm around my shoulders.

'Fine. Back of the net.'

'You seeing your father?'

I can't explain. 'Maybe after the game. Maybe for the weekend.'

'Good. Just let me know, right.'

'He's got a new friend.'

Mum laughs but I can sense that she's hurt. 'Lucky old Dweeble.'

'It won't last. Never does.'

'I don't care who your father sees.' But she does.

'Yeah. Think I'll get an early night.'

'Big day tomorrow.'

Too right. Big day tomorrow.

# CHAPTER 16

## I wanted to be me again . . .

. . . for those first few moments when I awoke the next morning. Stay in bed, get up late, wander on down to the game with Callan and Angie. Be a fan, be a spectator.

After all, I thought as I lay there, who would know any better? Lazlo would soon be forgotten as one of those quirks of football history. If Steve Malcolm wanted to investigate the boy who visited him, apparently with news from Lazlo, he would never find me. And City? City would be back next season, still there, still our team.

And out of the Premier League.

I groaned. There was no escaping what I had to do. I got dressed quickly and went downstairs.

I had almost finished breakfast when Mum

appeared in the kitchen, bleary-eyed in her dressing gown.

'What's going on?' she asked. 'It's Saturday. Why are you up so early?'

I fixed her with a Lazlo stare. 'I have a date with destiny.'

'Very funny, Stan.' She yawned. 'Well, I have a date with my bed. Can you bring me a cup of tea – before your date with destiny, if possible?'

I glanced at the kitchen clock. I had promised Steve Malcolm I'd be at the club by ten. Somehow I didn't think he'd accept talking to my mum as an excuse.

The kettle seemed to take about an hour to boil. I shoved a tea bag into a cup, splashed in some water, followed by some milk. By the time I reached my mother's bedroom, there was more tea in the saucer than in the cup.

'Beautifully served, Stanley,' she said, sitting up in bed.

'I'm going round to Callan's. We need to do some homework before the match.'

'Homework? Come on, Stanley, I'm not that green.'

'All right, I want to get in the mood for the match. I'll just fetch my boots.'

'You're not taking your boots again?'

'Mum, I've got to go.'

'But why take boots to a game?'

'You never know. They might need a spare player.'

'Stay and talk for a while. We haven't talked all week.'

'Later, Mum. After the game.' I kissed her.

'Boy oh boy, do I hate football.'

'It'll be on the radio. Remember to listen.'

'I won't.'

'Please, Mum. Listen out for Lazlo and pretend it's me.'

I left her shaking her head. 'Roll on the cricket season,' she said.

My boots and a stud key in a plastic bag, the magic stud in my pocket, I left the house. It was ten past nine. The ground was fifteen minutes walk away but there was the small problem of where I was going to do my Superman act and turn into Lazlo.

The plan was simple. Halfway down the High Street, there were some public toilets – the perfect place to change into a footballing superstar. I'd go in Stanley Peterson and emerge Lazlo. No problem.

I was feeling good now. I walked quickly down the road, my mind already fixed on the game this afternoon. I turned into the High Street, down the steps of the toilet. And stopped.

CLOSED DUE TO VANDALISM.

I closed my eyes as panic swept over me. Then I turned and ran up the steps. I looked at my watch. 9.20. I looked around wildly. A café? I had no money. Someone's house? Forget it.

Degsy's Sports Shop. Straight ahead of me. They knew me here. It was risky but I had no choice.

I walked in, sat down. Degsy, the owner of the shop, is one of those people who likes to chat to his customers. They say he was a bit of a hard man when he used to play for City – difficult to imagine when you looked at this bald, plump man in his fifties.

''Ullo, son. Ready for the big match, are we?'

Not exactly. 'Yeah.'

'They reckon that Lazlo's out of it. Saw a couple of the City lads last night. He hasn't been down there all week.'

'Football shorts, please.'

'Bloomin' foreign rubbish. If you want my opinion, we should ban foreign players – encourage our young lads for a change. Get your Lazlo down to play Wimbledon and get kicked around in the mud on a wet November afternoon – then we'd see whether he was any good.'

I looked at the time. 9.27. 'Shorts, Mr Degsy. It's urgent.'

He ambled over to the racks of shelves. 'Blue. White. Red. Adidas.'

'Red,' I said desperately.

Degsy wandered into the back room and disappeared for what seemed an age. 'Fresh out of red in your size,' he said, returning at last. 'They should play that Sturgess up front. Knows the formation, see. At the end of the day, it's all about—'

'Green, white – anything!'

Degsy stopped and gave me a long, cold stare.

Yes, now I could see why they called him the hard man.

'Please?' I squeaked.

He went into his storeroom and returned a few seconds later. He threw a black pair and a navy blue pair on the chair beside me. 'Changing compartment over there.' He nodded to a door in the corner of the shop.

Grabbing the shorts and my bag, I made my way across the shop and opened the door.

'Light switch is on the left,' Degsy called out.

I switched it on. Degsy's 'changing compartment' was what anyone else would call a largish cupboard, but it would have to do. 9.38. I took off my trainers, put them in the bag, pulled on my football boots and reached in my pocket for the activating stud.

I hesitated. From nowhere I heard my mother's words. 'The will fades like memory.' For a few precious seconds, I sat in the tiny room, concentrating with all my will-power and strength on City, on Lazlo. On the two hours at the City Stadium this afternoon when he would be king. I would be king.

I turned the stud in my boot. Nothing. Concentrate. Breathing deeply, my eyes squeezed shut, I turned again. Nothing. I tightened the stud and—

There was the merest split second of warning, of relief, before the power surged through me. It was quicker this time, and somehow I had managed to stay on my feet. My eyes closed in dread, I reached up slowly to touch my chin. My fingertips felt a

109

rough, hard stubble. I smiled, opened my eyes and looked in the full-length mirror.

Lazlo was back.

My watch had disappeared with Stanley Peterson but I knew that time was against me. Taking my plastic bag, I half-opened the door to the changing compartment. Degsy's back was turned. I made for the door. I was halfway there when—

'It's Lazlo!'

Behind me, from the direction of the storeroom, I heard the voice of Degsy's young girl assistant. 'Look at the shirt. No one makes Lazlo shirts yet. It's him.'

'Hullo, Lazza.' Degsy was advancing on me, hand outstretched. 'Derek's the name. Always been a great admirer of yours.'

'Oh yes?' Over the week Lazlo's gruff voice seemed to have dropped lower into his chest. His weird foreign accent was stronger than ever.

I shook Degsy's hand, then took the wrist of his left hand and turned it to see his watch. It was 9.50.

'Catch you later.' I turned and sprinted out of the shop.

Mistake.

I had forgotten two things. First I was back in the Lazlo Ferrari – when I sprinted now I was like lightning. And, second, I was in football boots.

As I reached the pavement and took a sharp turn,

I seemed to leave the ground for a moment, my legs pedalling in mid-air like something out of a Tom and Jerry cartoon. When I came down, it was my head that hit the pavement first.

# CHAPTER 17

## 'Can I have your autograph . . .

' . . . please, Mr Lazlo?'

'It can't be him, can it?'

'Can you hear me, Lazza?'

'You're meant to be up at the City Stadium, me old son.'

'Has he been out on the booze again?'

My head throbbed. I opened my eyes. Against a background of sky, a circle of faces were looking down at me.

'Stand back. He's coming round,' said a voice.

'What's the time?' I whispered.

'Just gone five to ten,' someone replied.

I groaned, and tried to struggle to my feet.

'Easy, Lazza. You've had a nasty knock.'

'Watch out, he's foreign.'

I stood up, holding my head. 'Got to get to the

Stadium,' I muttered, but the crowd pressed in on me, as if I wasn't a human being at all, but something that belonged to them all, something they wanted a share of.

I looked around desperately. Parked on the road, two yards away from where I stood, was a battered car. I pushed my way through to it and pulled open the passenger door. A young Asian guy looked across at me and smiled, as if this sort of thing happened every day.

'Where to, mate?' he said.

'Are you a cab?'

'I can be.' He laughed. 'Sometimes I am, sometimes I'm not.'

'City Stadium.' I pulled open the back door and jumped in. 'And it's kind of urgent.'

As the car drew away from the kerb, the voices of the crowd began to recede.

'You Lazlo, then?' The driver glanced at me over his shoulder.'

'Yeah.'

'Gonna score this afternoon?'

'Only if you get me to the stadium by ten.'

'No problem.' As the rackety old car gained speed, the driver reached into the glove compartment and took out a card which he passed over his shoulder to me. 'Rafiq,' he said. 'If ever you need a cab, give us a bell, mate.'

We were approaching the City Stadium. The

clock over the door read 9.59. I took a deep breath. 'Rafiq, I can't pay you,' I said.

'Eh? *Eh?*' For a second, I expected the car to screech to a halt, but Rafiq was laughing. 'Lazlo — and he's bloomin' skint. I've heard it all now, man.'

'I'll drop the money in.'

'Pay me with your feet this afternoon.' He braked sharply outside the main entrance. 'Go!'

'Cheers, Rafiq.' I jumped out of the cab and ran.

I burst into Reception. With a bored look, the City receptionist looked up.

'It's Lazlo,' I said.

As if I was just another of an endless string of people announcing that they were Lazlo, she picked up the telephone and slowly dialled a number. 'Tell Steve he's here,' she said.

# CHAPTER 18

## At the end of a long boardroom table . . .

. . . the manager stood in his City tracksuit. He was talking in a low voice to his squad of players who were seated on each side of the table. If it hadn't been for the football which now and then the boss bounced on the table in front of him, we might have been in a business meeting.

From the other end of the table, I watched the football, my mind focusing on the task ahead of me.

There had been a stir around the table when Joe Smith showed me in. Someone muttered, 'Oh 'ullo, wonder boy's back.' Steve Malcolm had paused in his speech. Then, as if my arrival was no surprise to him, he nodded unsmilingly in the direction of an empty chair at the end of the table. 'Take a seat, Geronimo,' he said.

Now he was talking about the game ahead of us and, to judge by the players' faces, they had heard it before. Liverpool's strengths – 'They're not an outstanding team, just an efficient one,' the boss said (oh yeah, we really believed that); their defensive weaknesses (he didn't mention they had conceded fewer goals than any other team in the League); the tactics we would be using.

He squeezed the ball in his hand as if checking whether it needed any more air, bounced it on the table again.

Now and then one of the other players darted a look at me. The captain Budgie Burton winked in a friendly way. Martin Sturgess, who seemed bigger and angrier than he had last week, stared ahead of him, chewing slowly.

After ten minutes, the manager's team talk drew to a close. 'Pitch practice and fitness tests in half an hour. Dinner twelve-thirty. Dressing room two.' He made as if to go, then paused. 'Oh yeah, and no phone calls to the press about our friend Lazlo.' He smiled in my direction. 'Some of you will have read stories in the tabloids about why he hasn't been in training. The fact is Lazlo and me, we've been in touch all this week. Eh, Lazza?' He narrowed his eyes as if daring me to challenge his story.

'Yeah, right,' I said. 'Boss.'

'There were reasons for him not training with us. Security reasons.'

I nodded, then looked along the row of faces on

116

each side of the table. Then stupidly, without thinking, I asked a question – *the* question.

'Am I starting the game, boss?'

There was silence in the room. Sturgess stared at the ceiling, a little smile on his face. Even before the manager started speaking, I knew I had made a bad move.

'The team announcement will be at two o'clock, as usual.' The manager spoke slowly and quietly. 'Everybody in this room knows that. All the reserves know that. Even the bloomin' tea ladies know that. It's the way we do things at City Football Club. Unless you think special rules apply for you.' He stared at me, as if expecting some kind of reply.

'I just thought—'

'You *thought?*' The manager looked around the table as if he couldn't believe what he had just heard. 'But you're not here to think, Mr Geronimo. You're here to do what you're bloomin' told. I do the thinking. It's what I'm paid for.'

I shrugged but, in the pit of my stomach, I felt a clenched knot of rage.

The manager wasn't finished with me. 'And where do you *think* you should play, Mr Geronimo?'

'Striker, boss?'

'So you weren't actually listening to my talk a moment ago.'

'Maybe he no speaky de lingo, boss.' Martin Sturgess spoke up. Beside him, Billy Dean laughed.

'Shut up, Martin.' The manager's eyes were fixed

on mine. 'What I said, Geronimo, was that Liverpool were vulnerable to crosses from the byline. Obviously that means we need someone good in the air up-front. Someone tall . . .' He glanced briefly in Sturgess's direction. 'Not a scruffy little shortarse like you. It's the team that matters.'

I closed my eyes, willing myself to remain quiet. Sturgess up front. It was crazy. The guy was tall. About ten years ago, he had been good with his head. But the spring had gone from his legs. His timing was out so that he was always in the right place but a split second too late. Every City fan knew that. In spite of all my efforts, a sort of growl emerged from me.

Steve Malcolm leant forward, both hands pressing the football into the table in front of him. 'Did you say something, Geronimo?'

There was nothing I could do. This time the growl contained a word. 'Lazlo.'

'Eh? What?'

'The name's Lazlo. Please let me start the game, boss. I can win it for you.'

The manager threw the ball at me and slapped the boardroom table with the palm of his hand. 'The strike force will be Dodd and Sturgess,' he snapped. 'Comprende, amigo?'

I stared at the football in my hands. It was my world. It was the only reality that mattered to me.

'Yeah, boss. Comprende,' I said.

'He has to pick on someone.' Budgie Burton walked beside me as we took to the pitch for the morning warm-up. 'I don't know whether it's nerves or some kind of management thing but, whenever there's a big game, he'll give someone a hard time that morning.'

'He thinks he's so great,' I muttered angrily.

'The press call him "the Mr Nice Guy of Football". If only they knew.'

I shook my head, still unable to believe what had happened. After everything I had done to bring Lazlo to life, I had forgotten that the best computer in the world couldn't change human nature. For some reason, Steve Malcolm didn't like Lazlo. And Lazlo had been unable to keep his mouth shut. It was beginning to look as if the footballing superhero could be watching the Liverpool match from the dug-out.

'Will he play me?' I asked Budgie.

'Not to start with. He's not one to change his mind, old Steve.'

'Substitute?'

'Don't count on it.' He gave me that familiar wink. 'There's always next season.'

I stared across the empty stadium. 'Me and my big mouth,' I said.

Standing beside me, Budgie looked at me with real curiosity. 'What was all that about this week?'

'It's sort of private,' I said. 'You know, family problems.'

'Got kids, have you?'

I wasn't ready for this one. 'Yeah, two. Son and daughter.'

'Nice. What are their names?'

My mind raced. 'Er, Callanoff and Angieoff,' I said. 'They're great kids.'

Budgie Burton gave me the sideways look of someone who's not sure whether he's having the mickey taken. 'Which one's the Popeye fan?' he asked suddenly.

'Popeye?'

'I noticed in the changing room that you had a Popeye sticking plaster on your arm.'

I smiled. It was true that the only sign of Stanley Peterson that had remained with me after I became Lazlo was the jokey plaster Dr Barber had stuck on me after giving me an injection. 'That's Callanoff,' I said. 'He thinks it brings me luck.'

'Hope he's right, old Callanoff,' said Budgie.

At two, in the dressing room, the manager announced the team. Dodd and Sturgess were up-front. No Lazlo. He read out the substitutes. No Lazlo. He folded the paper and put it in his tracksuit. 'Oh yes,' he said. 'Last substitute – Lazlo.'

I looked down, not daring to look at him for fear I would say something. I reminded myself that the game was the only thing that mattered.

I breathed deep into my lungs. Lazlo was ready. If he was allowed to play, he would be ready.

No if. No allowed. No would. Lazlo was ready.

'All right, Mr Lazlo?' There was mockery in the manager's voice.

'Back of the net, boss,' I said.

Fifty-five minutes later, we stood in the tunnel, two teams facing the most important game of the season. There was no talk, no jokes. The muffled buzz of a packed stadium was ahead of us. 'Let's go, lads.' Steve Malcolm looked around. We advanced like soldiers going into battle.

# CHAPTER 19

## Standing on the pitch . . .

. . . was like being within a great cauldron while, all around you, swirled feelings of tension, fear, hope, desperation and anxiety. Every Saturday afternoon was like that at the City Stadium, but this was different. This was unique.

Lazlo looked down to the visitors' end of the stadium where thousands of Liverpool fans, wave upon wave of red shirts, were gathered, confident that within two hours they would be cheering their side to the greatest prize in Club football. On the other three sides were the City fans, in their red and white, many of them waving flags, as if this wasn't the last desperate throw of the dice but a glorious Cup Final. There was a sort of drunken gaiety to them – their chants were too loud and fast, their laughter had an edge of desperation to it. It was a party – this, after all, could be our farewell to the Premier League – but no one was having fun. The next ninety minutes were too important for fun.

The warm-up passed quickly. I took my seat on the substitutes' bench behind the manager.

It was the moment of truth.

This game was never going to be a classic. Both sides were too afraid of losing to take the chances involved in clever football. Skill meant risk. Subtlety could wait until another day. This afternoon, only the result mattered.

Within moments the pattern of the game was set. Liverpool's fear of defeat meant they kept the ball, pushed forward, played short passes, building up their attacks with dogged patience.

City's fear of defeat meant panic. We lunged in, we chased the game, we mistimed our tackles. It was as if the defence wanted nothing to do with the ball, hoofing it upfield whenever it came near them, while the midfield could never keep it for long, chasing around the pitch like dogs chasing a tennis ball. The strikers were hardly in the game.

Even before Liverpool scored, Steve Malcolm had been up and down off his seat, screaming at the players, waving his arms about, adding to their anxiety. There had been three City bookings – Dean, Whitcroft and Stringer. And even before Liverpool scored, the City supporters knew with that sixth sense of the fan what was going to happen.

Then it happened.

A simple move. Midfield, wing, cross, lay-off. Field seemed to have the ball covered, but he didn't. In goal, Gary Peters dived, got a touch to the ball, but merely palmed it into the back of the net.

Goal, a split second of disbelief while every City fan was praying that it was a bad dream, that the ball had really missed and gone into the outside netting, that a linesman might be flagging for offside. Then the roar from the Liverpool fans confirmed the horrible truth.

Ahead of me, Steve Malcolm seemed to be having some kind of fit. He stood on the touchline, writhing and punching the air as if he were in a wrestling match with a ghost no one else could see. Fifteen minutes gone and the City team took up their positions with the weariness of condemned men.

The good teams, the great teams, don't behave normally when they go ahead. They don't shut up shop and defend. They've wounded the opposition and are like sharks who have tasted blood. They go for the kill. The eleven players in the red and white of City must have known that, but suddenly they were victims and could do nothing to save themselves.

Their minds were still on the disaster when it became a calamity. Wilson, Liverpool's big striker, was advancing on the defence. They were watching him, mesmerized, when O'Reilly made a run to his right. Wilson threaded the ball to O'Reilly between

Whitcroft and Field, who lifted their right arms for offside like puppets in perfect unison. They looked across at the linesman. Who kept his flag down. O'Reilly had timed his run perfectly. He took the ball around the keeper, then scampered it into the net with a mocking, triumphant little run like a small boy playing on a beach.

The City fans screamed with rage. Budgie Burton stood in front of the linesman and screamed abuse at him. Had O'Reilly been offside? Who knew? Who cared? The referee was pointing at the halfway line. The goal stood.

Now the clock accelerated in the way that can only happen in a football match when your team is losing.

Sitting in the dug-out, I remembered what Angie had told me about Liverpool. Not once this season had they surrendered a lead. Teams had managed to squeeze out a draw against them having been behind but they had never actually overtaken them. They kept possession, letting the opposition tire itself out. With every Liverpool pass, their fans gave a happy, taunting cheer.

Steve Malcolm was slumped on his seat. The City fans were eerily silent. Defeat was in the air that we breathed.

Or, rather, in the air that they breathed. I sat still, no longer thinking of the fans, or City, or Liverpool, or the occasion. I concentrated on the ball, on what

I would do to it. I breathed in deeply. I felt strong – more than strong. I felt superhuman.

*Lazlo.*

At first, it wasn't so much a chant that came from the Loft End but a whisper, a wish carried on the breath of a few hundred City fans gathered behind Gary Peters' goal. Liverpool supporters clapped at this sign of life from the opposing fans.

*Lazlo.*

The word came louder, the question becoming a statement, a demand. Some of the crowd on the far side of the stadium joined in. I became aware that all eyes were on me, willing me to stand up, get stripped off.

*Lazlo.*

Steve Malcolm stirred in his seat. The clock on the scoreboard showed that, unbelievably, there were only two minutes left in the first half. Tell the manager what to do and he would do the opposite – it had been true when journalists had tried to tell him which players to select. Would it be true of his own fans?

*Lazlo.*

It was as if the game was no longer relevant, as if only one thing mattered. Briefly, when Liverpool's central defender brought down Dodd outside the box, the chant died down. Burton took the free kick. It soared over the Liverpool crossbar.

*Lazlo!*

126

The rhythm was faster now, impatient, desperate. Laughing, happy, the Liverpool fans began to reply.

*Who?*

*Lazlo!*

The City fans weren't to be put off.

*Who?*

*Lazlo!*

*Who?*

The chant and its answer were speeding up. Even the players seemed to be distracted.

*Lazlo!*

*Who?*

*LAZLO!*

As the referee blew the half-time whistle, the chant lost its rhythm, fracturing into thousands of discordant voices, screaming, shouting, begging Steve Malcolm to bring me on.

The manager stood up, his face pale, his eyes bloodshot. He glanced at me. 'See you've brought the family,' he said, unsmiling, as he made his way down the tunnel towards the dressing room ahead of the players.

The team needed lifting but the manager seemed determined to destroy what self-belief they had left. All the poise, the cool, the confidence that he showed when being interviewed on television had suddenly deserted Steve Malcolm.

The team needed to be reminded that a game wasn't over until the final whistle blew, that they weren't down yet. What they got was anger, anxiety, a panicky sort of sarcasm.

The team were tired as only a team forty-five minutes from relegation at the end of a long season could be. And Steve Malcolm made them worse than tired. Depressed, they wanted it to be over, gone. They wanted to go home, get drunk, forget about football.

I sat in silence as the manager paced up and down, criticizing the players one by one. Even Robbie Field who was lying on the physio's bench having his right thigh massaged was told he wasn't trying hard enough.

'Boss, I'm not sure this hamstring's holding up.'

'Has it gone?'

Field shook his head. 'I can run but I'm saving it.'

'Saving it? You're all saving it,' said Malcolm, turning angrily on the team. 'Give it a couple of minutes in the second half,' he said to Field. 'If necessary, I'll bring on Andy Burgess.

The young full-back substitute clenched his fists.

Above our heads we heard the muffled chant of the fans. Each of us knew whose name they were chanting.

Darren Stringer lifted his head and asked if anyone had heard the scores from the other games.

'Never mind that!' snapped Steve Malcolm. 'All you need to know is that a draw isn't enough. We need at least three goals in the second half.'

Three goals. Against the mighty Liverpool. Who would be champions if they held on to their lead. The sheer hopelessness, the impossibility of the task flooded through each of us in that changing room.

'Coventry and West Ham are winning,' muttered Budgie Burton. 'One of the Liverpool fans shouted the score-lines to me as I was taking a corner.'

The door opened. It was time for the second half. I dared to look the manager in the eye.

He turned away.

'Don't let the crowd get to you,' he called out to the players. 'They know nothing.' He stared at me. 'Nothing.'

The second half picked up where the first half had left off – Liverpool confident, playing with the swagger of would-be champions, City edgy and rushed. There was a roar from the crowd when Joe Smith stood up and reached for the substitute board, followed by a groan when Andy Burgess began stripping off.

They actually booed him as he took to the field. The chant had started again. *Lazlo. Lazlo. Lazlo.*

Ten minutes gone. Joe Smith said something to the manager. He was pointing at Kevin Miller who was limping slightly. Steve Malcolm seemed to think for a moment, then nodded. Joe looked over his shoulder. 'Warm up, lad,' he said almost casually to me. 'You're on.'

Suddenly the fans were alive again, calling my name as I sprinted down one side of the pitch, did some stretching exercises. I returned to the dug-out. There was a roar, part relief, part excitement as I stripped off my tracksuit. Joe Smith stood up, the substitute board showing 15, Miller's number, in his hand. The ball seemed to stay in play for minutes as I waited beside the linesman.

Then it went out for a City goal kick. The referee noticed Joe, and so did Kevin Miller. He jogged to where I stood, smiled and shook me by the hand. 'Time for a miracle, Lazza,' he said. The linesman checked my studs, nodded.

Thirty minutes of the season left. Three goals needed. Against Liverpool. Miller was right – it was time for a miracle.

'City substitution,' the announcer's voice announced coolly. 'Coming on for number 15, Kevin Miller . . .

# CHAPTER 20

### 'Number 24, Lazlo . . .'

. . . An explosion of hope seemed to rock the City Stadium to its foundations as I sprinted on to the pitch.

I took up my position beside Georgie Dodd. He screamed something at me which I couldn't hear above the deafening, pulsating roar which vibrated in the bright, dense air around us.

But Lazlo plays his own game. I looked around the City players. The crowd may have been lifted but the team still had the empty, expressionless eyes of the walking dead. Then I saw the Liverpool players. In their mind, they were already champions. They had begun to play with the casual arrogance of superstars putting on an exhibition. They flicked the ball to one another, dummied and passed the leaden-legged City players. They were relaxed, triumphant, happy.

And foolish.

The ball was anchored in the City half. Whenever it was cleared out of defence, it fell at the feet of Liverpool players. They seemed about to set up an attack, but then took the ball out to the wings, passed it around, wasted more time.

I had waited long enough. Football is a team game but, when your team are playing like zombies, you have to break the rules. I moved out of position, jogging back from the halfway line, distantly aware of a weird rumble of anticipation from the City fans all around the ground.

O'Reilly was in possession for Liverpool, thirty yards from Gary Peters in goal. I knew his next move. He would look up as if about to send a power-drive of a shot at goal. As our defence tensed, he would drop his shoulder then pass it out to the left where Norstedt and Charles were wandering forward like a couple out for a Sunday walk in the park.

The Liverpool fans behind the City goal saw me. With one warning voice, they screamed, 'Man on!' Too late. I hit the accelerator.

O'Reilly drew back his right leg, hesitated, dropped his shoulder, brought down his foot.

But the ball wasn't there any more.

Play the way you're facing. I passed the ball to Dave Whitcroft and spun around racing upfield for the return. Don't hoof, pass. Whitcroft kept his head, sent a perfectly weighted ball into my path. I took it up, gained speed.

Darren Stringer seemed to have found new life in his legs and was sprinting to my left. I jinked, feinted a pass to him, but kept the ball. When Holdsworth went in to tackle me, he found himself facing air. I was gone. Noticing that Darren had strayed into an offside position, I paused, allowing him to pull back.

And allowing Brian O'Reilly to catch me just outside the area. He was angry. Seconds earlier, Lazlo had made him look stupid. Now Lazlo was going to pay – in pain. I saw him launching himself at me, feet first. With perfect timing, I took a side step, dragging the ball back. O'Reilly flew past like a jet crash-landing. I pushed the ball to my right, then let fly. Low, fast. Pechnik was just starting his dive as the net behind him bulged.

There was a sort of deep *whoomph*, like a vast bonfire catching light, as the crowd reacted. Darren Stringer had his arms around my shoulder. There was no time to waste in celebrations. I sprinted to get the ball, and before Pechnik could use up a few more seconds of the game, I grabbed it from the back of the net, and sprinted back to the halfway line, screaming at the City players as I went.

Now there was a game on. The Liverpool physio was on the touchline shouting something in Gary Fenton's ear. It wasn't instructions, I knew that – it was news from the other games at the top of the League. The Liverpool bench, I guessed, had heard that Newcastle were being held to a draw by Wimbledon – which meant that Liverpool had to win this game to be champions. If the score stayed at 2–1, it would be enough. And we had to win to save ourselves. Nineteen more minutes. Two goals.

Something about the atmosphere, about the way Lazlo had scored his goal, seemed to have destroyed Liverpool's rhythm. One moment, they had been strolling towards a championship, the next a City player had shattered their defence and scored. It had been our first shot at goal of the entire match, and they knew it wouldn't be the last. A sort of fear, a realization that the unthinkable could happen, seemed to enter their play.

City had changed, too. Lifted by Lazlo, urged on by the crowd. It was as if the will-power of 25,000 City fans had sent new strength into their muscles, hope into their hearts. Now they were first to the tackle. When the ball came loose, it seemed to be attracted as if by magic to a City boot.

I played it cool for a couple of minutes, letting Liverpool forget Lazlo. City were on the attack. A couple of Liverpool players, Charles and Fenton, tracked me around for a while but, as we pushed forward, they were forced to take up their usual position in defence. I jogged around in the midfield area, waiting for my moment.

Budgie Burton was in possession. He glanced

back to me. I held up my hand. Not me, not now. Down the right wing, the fleet-footed, dark figure of Ally Benson could be seen. Budgie chipped the ball over the Liverpool left back's head, allowing Ally to use his speed to keep the ball in play. Fenton turned to face him, crouching, holding back, like a cornered cat. The next move I knew. Push to the byline, double back and – I was on my way now – on to the left foot for a far-post cross.

Aim for space. Don't follow the ball. Look for the spot in the penalty area where it should arrive. Anticipate.

It wasn't the greatest cross from Ally Benson. There was a groan of impatience from the City fans as they saw it go too deep, too far beyond the City goal. But then the groan seemed to die in their throats as, for an instant, only two things seemed to be in motion on that pitch – the ball, hanging in the air, over the head of Alan Holdsworth, beyond the reach of Ian Pechnik.

And Lazlo.

Ten yards out from goal, I launched myself. The timing was perfect. As my forehead made contact with the ball, I twitched my head to the right with all the strength in my neck muscles. I saw it heading towards the far post before I crashed to the ground. The roar of the crowd told me all I needed to know. Bodies fell on top of me in an ecstasy of excitement.

Seconds later, I had pushed them off. Clenching both fists, I jogged back to the halfway line.

2–2. The result neither side wanted. Not enough for Liverpool to be champions. Not enough to save City from relegation. It was a question of whose nerve held in these last six minutes.

Five minutes. Four minutes. Three minutes.

I had a permanent escort of two Liverpool players now. Whenever I came near the ball, the stadium erupted. Liverpool were alive again, pushing forward. I stayed in midfield, pulling my two markers out of position but, while Liverpool were attacking, the position of their defenders made no difference to anything.

Norstedt was taking the ball down the left wing. He found O'Reilly in the centre. The Irishman ran at Billy Dean – and suddenly I saw what was going to happen. Fenton had run crossfield from right to left. He was unmarked. I moved. The ball arrived at Fenton's feet, seven yards from goal with only the keeper to beat.

The keeper and Lazlo.

With one last desperate lunge, I reached the ball a millisecond before Fenton. He sprawled dramatically and it seemed that the whole stadium was screaming for a penalty. I looked to the referee. He was surrounded by Liverpool players. He milked the moment for all its drama, then pointed to the corner.

I glanced at the clock. We were on full-time as O'Reilly sent in his usual inch-perfect corner. Gary Peters launched himself into a pack of players, fisting the ball away.

To me.

One of my markers, Charles, was with me but the other, Fenton, had gone up for the corner. I nutmegged the defender and set off through the heaving wall of sound that was now the City Stadium.

Chip the keeper? He was back on his line. Injury time was ticking away. To my right I saw the gangling untidy figure of Martin Sturgess. I never knew he could move that fast.

Norstedt was blocking my path. I could beat him but maybe I couldn't beat the clock. There was nothing for it. I passed the ball to Sturgess.

One on one. Dying seconds. How many times in the past had I seen Sturgess balloon the ball over the crossbar? I was five yards behind him when he hit it. Pechnik dived to his right. The crossbar seemed to crack as it made contact. It bounced out to me. The keeper was down, the goal gaping ahead of me.

I stroked the ball to Sturgess.

Who side-footed it into the net.

I was flying. Along the goal-line, leaving the rest of the team to mob Martin Sturgess, past the corner flag, up the touchline. Flying, my arms outstretched, my eyes half closed, the crowd a bright blur of faces, of hands reaching out. I stopped by the family stand, searching for Callan and Angie, looking for Dad, for anyone else I knew whose life I had just changed.

Two arms were reaching out for me from the

front now, a voice screaming my name. I stepped forward to shake a hand. And the arms were around me, pulling me forward, people laughing. A face above me. Hair, blonde hair, all over the place. A woman's voice, somehow familiar, was shouting 'You did it, Lazlo, you did it!' The arms pulled me towards the crowd and, before I could escape, kissed me on the lips, holding me, trapping me. I pulled back and, for a moment, the arms held me tight. Then I looked to see who the crazed kisser had been.

And found myself staring into the tear-filled eyes of Miss Tysoe.

'Miss——?'

'I love you, Lazlo.' Miss Tysoe seemed to be laughing and crying at the same time. 'I want to have your babies!'

'My . . . my what?'

'I'll have your babies, too.' An old man standing behind Miss Tysoe reached out a hand to me.

Distantly aware of the referee's whistle being blown furiously behind me, I rubbed my lips with the back of my hands, unable to move.

I had actually been snogging my teacher! On the lips!

For some reason, the Liverpool fans were booing me. The referee sprinted over to me, reached into his top pocket and held a yellow card over my head.

'Wha——?' I shook my head disbelievingly as Lazlo's name went into the referee's book for the first and last time. 'But ref,' I started trying to explain. 'She's my—'

'Time-wasting,' shouted the ref. 'Any more of that and you're off.'

My legs weak with embarrassment, I jogged back into position. Play restarted.

Liverpool advanced towards us. Eleven City players held back. Every second of a game counts. A championship can be won, a relegation issue decided, with the last kick of the game.

In a desperate last throw, Liverpool's defence were over the halfway. Pass, pass, pass. Nearer and nearer the penalty box. The referee looked at his watch. It was Holdsworth who cracked under the pressure. A full 35 yards from goal he let fly a scorching shot which flew twenty foot over the crossbar. Slowly, slowly, the ball was returned by the City fans. Casually, Gary Peters prepared to take the goal kick.

He hooked it high in the air. It soared towards the Liverpool half. As it began its descent, three long blasts of the whistle could be heard. The referee pointed two arms to the tunnel. Near me, Steve Charles sank to his knees in despair as a great roar of relief rose up from the City fans.

They were standing now, chanting, clapping. One or two broke through the cordon of stewards and policemen to leap around the pitch like crazed monkeys before being persuaded to return to their seats. Budgie had his arm round my shoulder. Tears were pouring down his cheeks. 'We did it,' he was repeating, again and again. 'I can't believe it, we did it.'

Steve Malcolm was on the pitch followed by two TV cameramen. Victorious, he was once again the kind, generous manager the world knew. He consoled Liverpool players who were slumped despairingly on the turf. He shook our hands one by one, saving a special hug for me – as if I had always been his favourite player. He stood on the centre spot, clapping the crowd, hands above his head. Mr Nice Guy.

From one side of the ground, there was silence. The Liverpool fans stood in blank, unbelieving despair, motionless like a still photograph. As their team made its way down to them, the crowd slowly came to life. They sang, 'You'll never walk alone', arms above their heads.

With Steve Malcolm and Budgie Burton at the head of us, we jogged a lap of honour. My eyes scanned the crowd for Callan, Angie or my dad. When I passed Miss Tysoe, I was too embarrassed to look at her. We reached the Liverpool fans. They clapped us with genuine feeling. We were all in it together.

Someone tapped me on the shoulder. It was Martin Sturgess. He held out a hand. 'Cheers, Lazza,' he shouted. 'Thanks for that.'

I smiled. 'Back of the net,' I said.

It was the perfect moment. The sun shining. Limbs aching with effort. Thousands of City fans already dreaming of Premier League football next season. Saved.

And Lazlo? To tell the truth, I felt less like Lazlo with every second. Suddenly, this wasn't my place – on the pitch, acknowledging the cheers. I wanted to be up in the stands, punching the air, singing along with the crowd, reliving every moment of the match with Callan and Angie.

The team were setting off on another lap of honour. Heads down, the Liverpool players were heading for the tunnel. It was time for Lazlo to make his last exit.

Ignoring the calls of my team-mates, I ran towards the tunnel.

'Eh, Lazza?' Joe Smith was standing by the dug-out. 'Where you off to?'

'Toilet,' I said.

Down the tunnel, left into the corridor leading to the home team's dressing room. No one there. I sat down, reached for my bag, closed my eyes. For a last few seconds, I listened to the stamping of feet above my head, savoured the atmosphere. *I'll remember this for ever.* I reached for the stud key.

Bye, Lazlo. Your date with destiny is over.

I lifted up my boot. My muscles were aching now. Maybe, if I was quick, I could find my dad at the exit to the paddock stand. Smiling, I held the stud key in my hand and turned my foot over.

It took several seconds for reality to sink in. I

was staring at the sole of a football boot with five studs.

The sixth had been sheared off during the game.

The magic stud was gone.

# TWO

# CHAPTER 21

## The champagne flowed . . .

. . . in the dressing room. There was laughter, joking, relief. The manager had become human again. For five minutes Roy Champneys, the chairman, had been there, full of pride and promises of money for next season. He made a little speech and mentioned my goals but, when he smiled at me, it seemed to me that there was a cold, moneyed look in his eye – the look of a farmer considering a prize pig just about to be sent to the market.

All this happened around me, but I wasn't really there. I felt dizzy, confused. Now and then I glanced down at my boot, as if to confirm what had really happened. If the stud had broken off in the game, how had I remained as Lazlo? In my mind's eye, I thought of the screen on Mum's computer. AFFIX

THE STUD, it had said. WHEN IT MAKES CONTACT,
YOU ARE LAZLO.

The contact was still there. And I was trapped in
the body of Lazlo. I looked down at my legs. Suddenly my muscles and bruises seemed scary, my
stubbly chin, the stupid, growly, foreign noise I made
when I talked – it all seemed like a sick joke, a bad
act that had gone on too long.

During the week before the game, I had looked
like Stanley, but had felt like Lazlo. Now it was the
other way round. To the world, I was Lazlo. Inside,
I was Stanley again.

'Cheer up, Lazza,' Robbie Field called across the
room. 'You look as if you've just been relegated.'

'No way,' I murmured. 'Back of the net.'

'It's all right, Mr Lazlo.' Steve Malcolm was
smiling but there was an insulting edge to his voice.
'We won the match, comprende?'

'Yeah, right. Cool.' I nodded.

'He's still thinking of that bird,' said Georgie
Dodd. 'I looked round after the goal. I was like,
"Where's Lazza gone, then?" And there he was,
snogging someone in the crowd.'

'It wasn't like that. She was my . . .' I hesitated.
'She's a sort of friend.'

'Photographers got it too,' said Darren Stringer.
'Mrs Lazlo's going to be well pleased.'

I stood up. 'I lost something on the pitch,' I said,
anxious to change the subject. 'A lucky bracelet.
Can I look for it?'

146

'You can look for anything you like, me old mate,' said Steve Malcolm, as if suddenly we were the best of friends.

I walked to the door.

'Coming to the party tonight?' Budgie Burton called out. 'We're all down at Result.'

'Result?'

'It's a club — a lot of the lads go there.'

'Yeah, maybe.' A thought occurred to me. 'I haven't got any clothes. I left them at home this morning.'

'We'll send someone round to fetch 'em,' said the manager. 'If you go out on the streets you'll get mobbed.'

'Er, no,' I said quickly, imagining Mum answering the door, showing someone from City into my room. 'Any chance of borrowing some?'

Malcolm laughed. 'I've got a spare suit in the office,' he said.

'Terrific,' I said, wishing I had kept my mouth shut. As if I didn't have enough problems, I was going to have to walk around in one of the manager's baggy, fashion-victim suits. 'Thanks, boss.'

I walked out on to the pitch. The stadium was empty now, with only a few stewards checking the stand for bags and jackets that had been left behind after the match.

It was strange. Days ago, it would have been a treat merely to walk on to the turf of City Stadium. Now all I wanted to do was to go home.

I checked first one goalmouth then the other. There was no sign of a small broken red stud. Then I tried the midfield areas. Nothing. It was a hopeless search. And, even if I did find the stud, it was broken. How was I going to take it out of the boot? Tears filled my eyes.

From the tunnel, I heard a whistle. The manager was there, some clothes over his arm. I walked over to him.

'There you go, Lazza.' Handing me a suit, shirt, socks and shoes, he looked more closely at me. 'You all right, mate?'

I wiped my eyes with the back of my hand. 'No problem, boss.'

'Find your bracelet?'

I shook my head.

'We'll get you another one.'

'Yeah.'

We entered the tunnel. To my surprise, he put a hand around my shoulder.

'Got an agent, have you, Lazza?'

'No. What's an agent for?'

Steve Malcolm laughed. 'For making you a lot of money, me old son.' He patted me on the back. 'I'll introduce you to someone tonight – someone who'll change your life.'

Yeah, like I really need my life changed even more. 'Thanks, boss,' I said.

He winked. 'The season's over,' he said. 'You can call me Steve.'

148

I wanted to get away, but where could I go? Call my dad? Go and see Angie or Callan? Wander home and say, 'Excuse me, Mum, but since you last saw me, I've turned into Lazlo.' Suddenly, my dream of becoming the football hero who saved the City had become a nightmare – a nightmare from which there was no escape.

Everyone wanted to meet Lazlo. After I had changed into the clothes Steve Malcolm had given me – consisting mainly of a sad white suit about three sizes too big for me – I made my way to the club's offices with the other players. More handshakes and hugs and kisses for the regular players. One middle-aged woman came up to me and kissed me on both cheeks. 'I don't know who the hell you are, darling,' she said. 'But I love you.'

'Back of the net,' I said.

A tall, thin, worried-looking man took me by the arm and led me to a corner of the room. 'Jamie Nicholls, City Press Officer, congrats and all that.' He extended a limp handshake. 'We've got a media feeding frenzy downstairs, and there's only one man they want to talk to. I suggest we do the television and radio first, then a press conference for the journalists.'

'No,' I said quietly. 'Interviews are lame.'

'I beg your pardon?' Nicholls was looking at me as if I had just insulted his mum.

I shrugged. Everyone was expecting me to act like Lazlo, the conquering hero, but suddenly I was tired of pretending to be someone I wasn't. If they didn't like the way I was, that was their problem.

'No need to get stressed out,' I said. 'I just don't want to give one of those sad post-match interviews. I'm over the moon, Brian. It just hasn't sunk in, Brian. All credit to the lads, Brian. It's all a load of old rubbish, isn't it?'

Nicholls lowered his voice. 'I don't know what your game is, mate, but I'll tell you this. If you don't talk to the press, they'll crucify you on the back pages tomorrow morning. It'll be all "Moody star sulks after big game" and "Lippy Lazza snubs faithful fans." '

'Big wow.'

'Eh?' Nicholls looked surprised.

'I said "Big wow". It's like major thanks, but no thanks.'

'Here's what we'll do.' Nicholls lowered his voice. 'No telly. No radio. No press conference, OK?'

I nodded.

'But . . . but just one in-depth interview with a journalist. A guy I know personally. Totally reliable. And maybe I can swing a couple of grand for you.'

'A couple of grand what?'

'Yeah, OK, you're right, you're worth more than that. I'll go for five grand. In fact, I think I can guarantee you five grand.'

'No way, José.' I smiled politely and moved away. Someone put a glass in my hand. Thirsty, I knocked it back. I spluttered as the drink hit the back of my throat, all tangy and powerful.

Beside me, Robbie Field laughed. 'Don't they have champagne where you come from, Lazlo?'

'Only at Christmas.'

'Where do you come from, by the way?'

'Flora Crescent,' I said. 'The house next to the newsagent.'

Robbie looked at me, his smile frozen on his face. 'Just because you scored a couple of goals, it doesn't mean you can take the mick, all right?'

'No way was I taking the mick.'

'You just watch that tongue of yours, Lazza.' Bunching his shoulders like a boxer before a fight, he turned his back on me.

I closed my eyes wearily. Everything I said suddenly seemed to anger people.

I felt a hand on my shoulder. It was Steve Malcolm. 'Suit all right, Lazza?'

I looked down at the clown's outfit I was wearing. 'Yeah. Cool.'

'There's more where that came from.'

Thanks, but no thanks. 'Great.'

'Cars. Cash. Holidays in the sun.' He nudged me. 'Women.'

'Back of the net.'

'That's if you play the game.' He grabbed a bottle of champagne from a table nearby and poured my glass to the brim. 'What's all this I hear about you refusing to do interviews?'

'Interviews are lame,' I said. 'I just find it really embarrassing.'

'Lame!' He laughed. 'I'd love to know where you learnt your English.'

'St Vincent Primary School. Miss Tysoe's class.'

'Great sense of humour! I like that in a player.' The manager put his arm around my shoulder and squeezed. He was surprisingly strong. 'Tonight I'll cover for you with the press — say you're a bit emotional after the game, a bit shy. Your English isn't so hot. Then tonight we eat dinner here, and on to a club later. I'm going to introduce you to someone who's going to make you a lot of money.'

'I don't want a lot of money.'

His hand squeezed harder, digging into my shoulder muscles. 'We all want a lot of money, Lazlo. Even if we think we don't, we do. Got a mother, have you?'

I thought of Mum and suddenly felt lonely and frightened. 'Yeah, I've got a mother.'

'You can buy her a house. Just like that. And a car.'

'We've got a house and a car.'

'A big car, Lazlo. But if you're not going to play the game the City way, there are always other clubs. You're a hot property now, son.'

'Great.'

'And, right now, you're a property that belongs to City Football Club. We're very proud of you. We want the very best for you.'

I nodded. The manager was smiling, looking deep into my eyes as if he was the most caring person in that room.

So why did I feel that what I had just heard had been a threat?

The evening passed in a haze. There was a dinner in the club boardroom. Speeches were made by the chairman, by the manager. To listen to either of them you would have thought that bringing Lazlo to the club had been the result of a plan so cunning and so brilliant that they weren't able to reveal the secret of how it was done.

Budgie Burton stood up to thank the lads, the manager, the chairman, his mum and dad. After a few seconds, it became clear that he was better at football than he was at making speeches. Some of the players pretended to fall asleep. When, at last, he reached the end of it, he made a presentation to Martin Sturgess, the club's longest-serving player and scorer of the goal that had kept City in the Premier League. Sturgess stood up and for a moment I thought he was going to cry. He held up the small cup he had been given and said, 'Yeah, cheers, lads. Say no more, right?' and sat down to wild applause.

Shrugging modestly, he glanced up at me and winked. I winked back.

Already I was learning lessons about life as Lazlo. The first was to keep quiet at all times. Everything

I had said before dinner had been misunderstood, so now I just grinned and nodded.

Now and then I caught some of the players looking at me with open curiosity. Lazlo could play football, they seemed to have decided, but, off the pitch, he wasn't too bright. When they talked to me, it was in slow, loud voices. 'Yeah,' I'd nod slowly as if I was really simple. 'Cool. Back of the net.'

But soon, too soon, the party broke up. A few of the players were going home. I was facing a decision. Wander off into the darkness or go along with the manager and some of the team to their favourite nightclub?

As if reading my mind, Steve Malcolm called across the table. 'Coming with us, Lazza?'

I shrugged uneasily. 'Not sure.'

'Course you are. Remember what I said earlier – about introducing you to someone?'

'He just wants to meet that girl he snogged in the crowd,' Darren Stringer shouted out.

Blushing, I nodded. 'I'll come along with you then.'

I didn't exactly have a choice. After all, where else could I go?

# CHAPTER 22

## Maybe it was the drink . . .

. . . but I felt more relaxed now. By the time I got into the back of Steve Malcolm's Jaguar with Budgie Burton and Robbie Field, I was almost beginning to forget that the real me was trapped inside Lazlo's body with no way of escape. The stud? Someone would find it in the morning. It occurred to me that it had been lucky I had told Callan that I was seeing my father – Mum would assume I was spending the weekend with him.

By Sunday night, I'd be home, Lazlo would be history and City would be in the Premier League for another season. Not a bad weekend's work by any standards.

In the meantime, there were celebrations to enjoy.

We drove into the centre of town and pulled up outside a small door in a dark street. As we stepped out, a huge man with cropped hair stepped out of the shadows, opened the car door for us, then ushered us into the club. Steve Malcolm flashed a large note in his direction. 'Get one of the lads to park the car for us, will you, John?' he said.

Yes, this was the life.

We went down some stairs and entered this big bar room where we were greeted by a blonde woman who looked as if she had just stepped out of a glossy magazine.

Steve Malcolm kissed her. 'Nice table for Lazlo and the lads,' he said.

Lazlo and the lads. That was how it was this evening. As we were taken to our table, I couldn't help noticing that people were nudging one another, muttering, their eyes following us across the room.

Is that . . .?

It's not, is it?

It is. It's Lazlo.

He's smaller than he looks on telly.

'This is a private club,' said Budgie, noticing my curiosity. 'Mostly sportspeople and actors. We won't get hassled here.'

He reckoned without Lazlo appeal. We had hardly poured our first glass of champagne when a girl with curly dark hair a bit like Miss Tysoe's and a short dress that Miss Tysoe wouldn't have been seen dead in, approached our table.

'May I join you?' she said to Steve Malcolm.

The manager pulled up a chair. 'Why not?'

'I'm Julie.' The girl smiled and put the chair next to me.

'Congratulations,' said Steve and turned to talk to Robbie Field.

Julie didn't seem to mind not being introduced. She extended a hand. 'Mr Lazlo, I presume,' she murmured in a low voice.

'How d'you do, Julie.' I shook her hand politely.

'How's the man of the match then?'

'Not . . .' I tugged at my hand and, after a brief struggle, Julie let me go. 'Not too bad, thank you,' I said.

A waitress appeared and placed another glass in front of her. She cleared her throat and looked pointedly at the bottle of champagne. Smiling, Budgie poured her a drink.

'Cheers,' she said, not taking her eyes off me.

'Nice club,' I said.

Although there was plenty of space around the table, Julie moved a bit closer. 'D'you prefer being called Lazza?' she asked.

'Lazlo,' I smiled. 'Lazza sounds a bit lame, doesn't it?'

'You know what I'd just love?'

I moved my chair away slightly. 'No.'

'Your autograph.'

'Oh. Fine. What shall I sign?'

She blinked her eyes at me in an odd way. 'What would you like to sign, Lazlo?'

'D'you have a bit of paper?'

For some reason, Julie seemed disappointed. She stretched across me to reach a napkin. 'Got a pen?' she asked Budgie.

'Bloomin' heck.' Budgie reached inside his jacket pocket and pulled out a biro. 'He's getting her telephone number – he's as fast off the pitch as he is on it.'

Embarrassed, I took the napkin. I've got really bad handwriting, so I wrote my name carefully, then gave it to Julie.

'Your writing ain't half funny,' she laughed.

'So?' I shrugged. 'Neatness is for girls, isn't it?'

Julie looked slightly surprised. 'Yeah, suppose it is.'

I noticed Steve Malcolm was looking at me across the table. 'Before you get . . . involved, Lazlo . . .' He gave a sort of leer. 'I need to introduce you to someone.' He stood up. 'He'll be five minutes,' he said to Julie.

I followed the manager past the bar. Next to a room where couples were dancing, there were a few alcoves with a table in each one. Steve Malcolm nodded in the direction of a table where a small, plump man with long hair was sitting talking to a woman. 'I'm introducing you to someone a bit special.'

'Yeah? Cool.'

'Cool is right, me old mate. That there is the one and only Terry Mills.'

'Yeah?'

'Don't tell me you've never heard of Terry Mills? Where have you been, Lazza?'

'Around. What's so great about Terry Mills?'

'He happens to be the most powerful agent in the country – sporting agent.' Steve Malcolm squeezed my arm. 'With Mills batting for you, you'll be in clover.'

'I don't really—'

But he was advancing on the table. 'Tel!' He stood in front of the table. Terry Mills stood up and the two men hugged. After a few seconds, Mills held Steve at arm's length, resting his pudgy little hands on the manager's shoulders.

'You did it, son. I knew you'd do it. And you did.' He shook his head, apparently too overcome by emotion to carry on. 'Your boys were superb.'

'I thought you were a Liverpool fan.'

'Liverpool Schmiverpool – I've always been a City man deep down.'

The manager extricated himself from Terry Mills' arms. 'Tel, there's someone you should meet.'

The agent stared at me and spread his arms as if a miracle was happening in front of his eyes. 'Unreal,' he said. 'Just unreal.'

'Eh?' I gulped nervously, for a moment thinking that Mills had somehow discovered my secret. 'Not really.'

Terry Mills bounded forward and pumped my right arm for several seconds. 'Magic stuff, Lazza, magic stuff. I have never seen skills like I saw on that park today. And I've been going to football all my life, seen all the great strikers. Best, Maradona, Romario – forget it. You rewrote the history books, mate.'

'Wicked,' I said.

'Wicked is right.' Mills showed me towards his table, waving away his woman companion as if she was a fly that had settled on a chair. Without looking at either of us, she stood up and moved away.

'Tell you what, I'll catch you guys later.' Steve Malcolm reached into his pocket and gave me a card. 'You may want to call me at home.'

Before I could ask him why on earth I needed his home number, he had given a little wave and was gone.

Mills poured a glass of champagne into an empty glass that was on the table and looked into my eyes. For a moment I thought he was going to burst into tears.

'I like your style, Lazza,' he said.

'Great.'

'Not just as a footballer, but as a bloke. I think we could be friends. Personal, like.'

'Yeah?'

'Let me ask you something, Laz. Right now, what d'you want most in the world?'

'Um . . .' To be back in Stanley Peterson's house, Stanley Peterson's bed, in Stanley Peterson's skin. That was the truth but somehow I didn't think Terry Mills would understand. 'I'm not sure, really.'

'Come on, Lazza. Big car – a Ferrari maybe? An island off the coast of Scotland? House for your mum and dad? A villa in the West Indies with hot and cold running girlfriends, eh?' He nudged me. 'Eh? Magic stuff.'

I looked across desperately to Steve Malcolm's table. The manager was in deep conversation with Robbie Field. Seeing me, Budgie Burton smiled as if he knew what I was going through. 'I suppose a Ferrari would be quite cool,' I said.

'Five.' Mills slapped the table. 'I'll get you five Ferraris tomorrow – one for each day of the week and maybe a Lear jet for the weekend, yeah? Ask me how, go on then.'

'Er, how?'

'Sign up with me and you'll be a millionaire by Wednesday. How about that then?'

'Yeah, that – that sounds very nice.'

'*Nice?*'

'Thank you very much.'

Terry Mills was giving me a suspicious sideways look. 'Here, you've not got an agent already, have you? You're not messing me about?'

'No.' I shook my head desperately.

'Because no one messes Terry Mills about, right?'

'Right. I know. And I'm not messing you about. Honestly. I don't even know what an agent is.'

Terry Mills was smiling again. 'An agent is like a Father Christmas who looks after you every day of the year.'

'Cool.'

Suddenly, as if he remembered he had an appointment elsewhere, he grabbed my hand and shook it. 'It's a deal then. Come to my office on Monday and we'll iron out the details.' He reached into his jacket pocket, pulled out a card, scribbled something on the back and handed it to me with a look of deep seriousness on his face. 'This is your ticket to a fortune, Lazza. Call me any time on Monday and I'll send a car round for you.'

I stood up. 'Yeah, and I'll definitely think about that.'

'*Think* about it?' It was a shout that made one or two people at the bar turn to look at us. 'We've shaken, Lazza.' He held out his hand as if it was a pistol. 'You breaka ze deal, I breaka your legs.' He laughed uproariously.

'Eh?'

'Only kidding.' But the smile, frozen on Mills' face, suddenly seemed a lot less friendly than it had been. 'Just don't talk to any other agents, right?' He shook my hand again. 'Deal?'

'Deal.'

As I turned to go back to the table, his woman friend appeared out of nowhere. She brushed past me rather too closely, looking into my eyes as if she was somehow trying to tell me something.

I must have looked a bit weird when I returned to Steve Malcolm's table because Budgie Burton said quietly, 'Don't worry about Tel. He'll make you rich as long as you stay on the right side of him. By this time tomorrow, he'll have talked to all the big clubs in Europe about you. Could be the biggest transfer in the history of football.'

'Transfer?' I snapped out of my daze. 'Who's talking about a transfer?'

Budgie smiled at my innocence. 'That was why the manager introduced you to Mills. He wants to cash in quick. The club needs the money and he gets a cut of any profit on the transfer market.'

'What about me?'

Budgie laughed. 'I thought you were a foot-baller. Didn't you realize? We're just a commodity – deal-fodder.'

'But . . .' I glanced across the table to where the manager was sitting. 'Why does Mr Malcolm want to get rid of me? I've just helped save the club from relegation.'

'You showed him up, didn't you? He may be acting friendly now but he wants you out.'

I closed my eyes. It had been a long day, my muscles ached, the champagne had made me feel sleepy and the news that I was part of some sleazy deal between Steve Malcolm and Terry Mills wasn't improving my mood either.

I felt a hand on my shoulder. I looked up and Julie was standing beside my chair. 'All right, Laz?' She smiled. 'You look like someone who'd rather be somewhere else.'

'Yeah, right.'

'Like where?'

'Like . . .' I gave a big sigh and rubbed my eyes. 'Like home.'

'All right,' said Julie. 'I'll just fetch my coat.'

# CHAPTER 23

## 'Where to, kind sir . . .?'

. . . Julie was sitting behind the steering wheel of
her car, a flash, black Golf with darkened windows.
It felt good to escape from Result back into the real
world and Julie seemed an understanding sort of
person, but now I faced a problem. Where to? I
wish I knew.

She started the car. 'Like, where d'you live?' she
asked.

'Um, there's something you should know.'

'Yeah?'

'It's a bit difficult to explain.'

'Oh right.' She gave a little laugh which somehow
made her seem much older and tougher than she
really was. 'It always is.'

'Is it?'

'Why don't you save the explanations until we're back at my place?'

Without waiting for my reply, she put the car into gear and accelerated away from the curb.

We raced through the dark streets, dance music blaring from the car's sound system. My head throbbed and I felt slightly sick. I had a nasty idea that we weren't going back to Julie's place to watch *Match of the Day* but right now it was good not having to talk, to pretend.

After about ten minutes, we drew up in this quiet street. Julie led me into a little house, so tidy it looked as if nobody lived there.

'Take a pew,' she said waving in the direction of a pink sofa.

'Back of the net,' I muttered, slumping down.

'Can I get you anything, Laz?'

'Just a Coke, please. Or anything soft.'

She went to the kitchen and came back with two glasses. She sat down really close to me on the sofa.

I held the Coke to my forehead, then put it in front of my face so that I felt the cooling bubbles on my nose. 'I love the way it tickles,' I said.

Julie looked at me as if there was something weird about Coke bubbles tickling a person's nose. 'Tell me about yourself, Laz.'

'It's boring.'

'Not for me it isn't.' She was burrowing towards me again. 'Like, for instance, who've you got at home, waiting for you?'

Tricky one. I couldn't exactly tell her it was my mum without giving everything away. 'There's this person,' I said carefully.

'Called?'

'Susan.'

'Your old woman, is she?'

'Not that old. She's only just forty.'

'Forty!'

'Yeah,' I laughed. 'She gets well stressed about that, too. She always says she's 38.'

'What about your friends?'

'There's this bloke Callan – he collects football stickers.'

'Oh. Oh, right.'

'Then there's Angie . . .'

'Girlfriend?'

'Angie? No way!' I had shifted down the sofa but Julie had followed me. Now she casually draped her arm around me. I felt her long fingernail tickling my ear. 'On the other hand, yes,' I said suddenly. 'Angie's my girlfriend. We're really serious about each other. In fact, it's true love.'

'So where's she now?' Julie whispered.

I shrugged. 'Her parents' place, I guess. Her mum doesn't like her staying out late.'

'You're having a laugh, aren't you.' Julie's fingers were messing up my hair. 'I like that in a man.' She stood up, stretched her arms and yawned. 'Well,' she said in a funny sort of whisper. 'It's long past my bedtime.'

'Mine too.'

'You must be tired.'

'You bet.'

'I'll be through there.' She gave me an odd smile. 'All right?'

'Yeah. Cool.'

She wandered out, turning the lights off as she went.

For a moment, I sat there in the half-darkness, wondering what to do next. I put my feet on the sofa, let my head rest on a cool cushion. I swear I've never wanted to sleep more in my life. I closed my eyes.

It was an odd sort of dream that I had that night. Someone was shaking me gently, trying to get me to stand up, whispering things, calling out Lazlo's name. I wanted to wake up, but I couldn't. It was as if my eyelids were glued together. Eventually the shaking stopped. And there was silence.

Sleep at last.

# CHAPTER 24

## Half-light, the sound of birds . . .

. . . and a throbbing inside my head awoke me the next morning. For a few seconds, I stared around me, confused as to why I was in this strange flat rather than my bedroom. I ran a hand over my chin.

And groaned. Thick stubble. Now I remembered.

I was Lazlo. With a hangover. In the flat of a girl I had only met once. Without the magic stud.

Terrific.

I sat up and, for a moment, I thought I was going to be sick. After a few seconds, I carefully put on my shoes which Julie must have removed after I had crashed out. I tiptoed into the kitchen, took a drink of orange juice from the fridge. A clock on the wall showed that it was just past nine.

I had to get out of there and was just about to

leave when I remembered Julie and how she had looked after me the previous night. She had been a bit strange, old Julie, but, if it hadn't been for her, I would probably still be at Result with Terry Mills and Steve Malcolm. From somewhere at the back of my aching brain, I seemed to hear my mother's voice telling me that good manners never hurt anyone.

There was a Snoopy message-board on the wall next to the fridge. I picked up the crayon that was attached to the board and, in my neatest hand-writing, I wrote:

*Dear Julie*
*Thank you very much for having me.*
*Love*
*LAZLO*

Quietly I let myself out of the flat.

Outside there was a pale spring sun in the sky but it was still cold. Pulling the jacket of my ridiculous white suit closer to me, I turned left and walked quickly down the street.

It was quiet – Julie seemed to live in some kind of suburb – but, after about five minutes, I came to a main road. On the corner was a news-stand. The old man who worked there looked at me as if he had never seen a person in a baggy white suit before.

'Excuse me, mate,' I said. 'Where am I?'

'Eh?'

I repeated the question but it seemed to be a bit

too complicated for him to take in because he looked first at the papers laid out in front of him, then back at me.

I glanced down and immediately understood the problem. On the front page of every paper was a photograph of Lazlo. On one, it was my diving header. Another showed me wheeling away, arms outstretched, after Martin Sturgess's goal. Several of them showed me in a heavy clinch with a girl in the front row of the stands. I groaned. Miss Tysoe. Talk about embarrassing.

'Are you . . .? You're whasname, aren't you?' the old man said at last.

'Not really,' I muttered, turning to walk away. 'Thanks for your help.'

'Bloomin' stuck-up snob.' His voice followed me down the street. 'He scores a couple of goals and he thinks he's the bloomin' Queen of Sheba.'

There were one or two cars passing by. Now and then their drivers would glance at me. In my dazzling, heavily creased white suit, I wasn't exactly blending in with the scenery.

Sinking my hands deep in my trouser pockets, I felt something that felt like a card – two cards, in fact. Deep in thought, I took them out. The first one read *TERRY MILLS, Personal Management* – there was no help there. I'd need to be in a lot worse trouble than this before I turned to old Terry.

I looked at the second card.

*RAFIQ TAXI SERVICE*
*Airport. Stations. Special Rates.*
*Service with a Smile.*

Rafiq. The guy who had taken me to the ground yesterday. There was a telephone kiosk nearby. I had no money but I remembered what to do from a school trip last year.

'I'd like to make a reverse charge call,' I told the operator. I gave her the number.

'Name of caller?'

'Lazlo. That's spelt L . . .'

'Like the footballer, right?'

'Yes. Like him.'

'What a goal, that header, eh?'

'Right. Back of the net, that was.'

There was a moment's pause as the operator rang through. I prayed that Rafiq would answer, that he would remember me from yesterday. For what seemed like minutes, there was silence on the line. Then I heard a familiar voice.

'Hey, two goals, man. You did it!'

'Yeah, I did it – thanks to you getting me there.'

'Saw your picture in the paper.' He laughed. 'Looked like you were enjoying yourself with that girl in the crowd.'

'Rafiq, I need help. I'm somewhere in London. I've got no money. It's . . . difficult to explain over the phone.'

'Lazlo needs help? You are weird, man.' He

laughed but, hearing my silence, he seemed to realize I was being serious. 'Give me the address, then.'

I looked across the road. There was a street sign opposite where I stood. 'I seem to be on Magdalen Road. In a telephone kiosk.'

'No problem.'

'You know it?'

'I'm a minicab driver, Lazlo.'

'Yeah, sorry. Back of the net, Rafiq.'

'I'll be ten minutes.'

As I hung up, I noticed for the first time that I was no longer alone. Two women were standing nearby, staring at me. I smiled and turned away.

'You're him, aren't you?'

I heard the voice of one of them behind me. I tried to ignore it.

'Hullo. *Hullo.*' The woman spoke more loudly. 'You're that bloke what scored the goals.'

I mumbled something.

'Give us your autograph, then.' The second woman pushed an old piece of paper and a pen at me. I signed it but, looking at the autograph, the woman seemed dissatisfied. 'Put "To Barry". That's my bloke.'

Smiling as politely as I could manage, I scribbled 'To Barry' above my name.

'He doesn't reckon to you, as it happens. Said that second goal was a fluke.'

I closed my eyes briefly. Right now, I didn't need this.

'Maybe he don't speak English,' said the woman's friend.

'My Barry says we only get the rubbish foreign players.'

'Moody, isn't he?'

'That's foreigners for you. Up and down. You never know where you are with a foreigner.'

I turned to face the two women. 'Please,' I said. 'Please leave me alone.'

'See what I mean?' They looked at one another as if I wasn't a person at all, but some kind of object.

'Just because you're famous, it doesn't mean you can't have a chat,' Barry's girlfriend called out.

'Here, Lazza, we'll leave you alone if you write something really nice for our friend Barry.'

I nodded wearily and held out a hand for the pen.

'You can put "I wish I could play football like Barry Finch."'

I wrote it, then handed back the piece of paper.

'You don't look half as good as you do on the telly,' said the first woman, making no move away. 'In fact, you look dead rough.'

'Yeah, he's really small, isn't he?'

They were still chatting about me as if I wasn't there when a few minutes later, Rafiq drew up in his taxi.

'Fans?' he asked as I got into the passenger seat.

'They were unbelievable. Just because they've seen you on TV, they think they can say anything they like.'

'Fame, who needs it?' Rafiq laughed. 'Where to?'

'City Stadium again. I have to pick something up – something important.'

But I was too late. The main entrance to the stadium was locked. Rafiq and I peered through one of the iron gates. A small tractor was going backwards and forwards on the pitch, harrowing up the grass.

Whatever chance there had been of finding the red stud that could save me from a life as Lazlo had now disappeared.

'I'm in trouble,' I said to Rafiq.

'Want to talk about it over dinner? My family has an Indian restaurant. Excellent food.'

Why not? It would give me time to think.

'That would be cool,' I said.

Rafiq's family didn't like football. Didn't watch it, didn't play it, weren't interested in who won the League or who was relegated. For all they cared, City Football Club might never have existed. As for me, I was just one of Rafiq's friends – a guy who didn't talk much but who liked his Indian food. It was great.

I sat at one end of a long table in the Far Pavilions Tandoori House. Every Sunday lunchtime, Rafiq's uncle closed his restaurant to the public and invited his family and their friends round for a meal that seemed to go on for hours with course after course. They were a friendly, relaxed crowd with children running under the table, everyone tucking into food, and Rafiq's uncle sitting at the head of the table, a big smile of contentment on his broad features.

'What will you be doing now that the football season is over, Mr Lazlo?' the uncle called down to me at one point.

I shrugged, racking my brains to remember what footballers normally did when they weren't playing football. 'Golf,' I said eventually. 'I'm well keen on golf.'

This seemed to satisfy my hosts and the conversation returned to family gossip.

As the afternoon wore on, I began to worry once more about what I should do next. The stud was gone. Soon Mum would realize that Stanley had gone, too. I could just turn up as Lazlo, but she wouldn't believe what had happened. Even if I could prove that I was Stanley, she'd be terrified.

There was something else bothering me. In spite of everything, I felt as if I was becoming more Lazlo and less Stanley all the time. Ever since I had woken up on Julie's sofa, I had found myself thinking of Stanley as if he was someone else, separate from me. For the first time, it occurred to me that maybe there was another solution to my problem.

If I could just explain everything to my parents and to Callan and Angie, and maybe to Miss Tysoe, maybe my future lay in being Lazlo after all. Money would be no problem. Even if Steve Malcolm sold me to one of the big clubs, I would never have to worry about my future. People seemed to notice me as Lazlo, listen to what I said. The life of Stanley Peterson, class nobody, would probably seem a bit tame beside that of City's own football superhero.

'What d'you think, Lazlo?'

'Hm, sorry?' I became aware that Rafiq was talking to me, that the people around the table were looking at me expectantly.

'We were talking about my sister Gita. She's fallen in love with this white guy. They've gone away for the weekend together.'

'She's only nineteen.' Rafiq's uncle shook his head.

'Nineteen's big,' his wife, sitting beside him, protested. 'It's not the age I'm worrying about. It's the man. Falling in love with a white boy – it's a disaster, I tell you.'

There was a babble of voices from around the table.

'It's not the way someone looks that matters.' Rafiq banged the table as he spoke. 'As long as he's honest.' He turned to me once more. 'Am I not right, Lazlo?'

Silence descended on the table.

I nodded slowly, thinking suddenly not just of Gita's boyfriend, but of me, of my future, of the choice I had to make between Lazlo and Stanley. 'That's right,' I said. 'You have to be true to yourself.'

'Has he got a decent job, prospects?' the aunt muttered gloomily. 'That's what I want to know.'

I leant over to Rafiq. 'Is there a telephone book here? I need to find someone's address.'

Thirty minutes later, he left me at the end of the road. It was almost five o'clock and, although the sun was still shining, there was a chill in the air.

'You all right here?' Rafiq looked concerned.

'I'm fine.'

'Call us and have a drink sometime, yeah?'

'All right, then.' I held out a hand. He laughed and shook it. 'Thanks for everything, Rafiq. I'm sorry about not being able to pay you.'

'Pay me back in goals next season.'

'I'll try.' I stepped out of the car and tapped on the roof. 'See you then.'

He gunned the car and, with a wave, was gone.

Number 35A. I made my way slowly down the street. This was going to be tricky.

I stood in front of the small, neat house, then walked up the path. There were two bells beside the door. I rang the one marked 'A' and waited. No reply. I rang again. Nothing.

Since there was no one around watching me, I made my way past the front window, down a side passage between the house and its neighbour. There was a wooden door at the end. I turned the handle. It was unlocked.

In front of me was a small garden. There were daffodils and primroses and purple flowers on each side of a tiny, square lawn.

# CHAPTER 25

## Kneeling on the lawn . . .

. . . in front of one of the flower beds, a trowel in her hand, was Miss Tysoe.

I cleared my throat and she started.

'Sorry,' I said. 'I didn't mean to give you a fright.'

The sun must have been behind me because she lifted her right hand to her eyes.

'It's me,' I said.

She stood up slowly. 'I don't believe it,' she murmured, self-consciously trying to wipe the dirt from her hands down the side of the baggy jeans she was wearing. 'What are you doing here?'

'Charming.' I tried to laugh but all that emerged from my throat was a weird, husky 'har-har'. I sounded like a sea bird.

'Lazlo?'

I nodded.

Hesitantly she put out her hand. 'I'm Gemma Tysoe.'

'I know – I mean, I'm pleased to meet you . . . again.' We both laughed, remembering yesterday.

It was beyond strange. At school, Miss Tysoe was always in control, the most confident person you could imagine. Now she seemed shy, lost for words. It was almost as if she was the little girl and I was the grown-up.

'What are you doing here?' she managed to say eventually.

I shrugged. 'I've got a problem. I thought you might be able to help.'

She gave me the sideways look she puts on in class when someone has come up with the lamest excuse for not doing homework. 'Help? How?'

'It's a bit of a long story.'

'We'd better have a cup of tea then.'

'Great.' I followed her into the house. 'Tea would be good.'

'Sorry,' she said casually as she pushed open the back door. 'The place looks like a bomb has hit it.'

We walked through a small kitchen into the sitting room. Usually when adults say a place is untidy, they mean a newspaper has been left on a chair or a lamp isn't quite straight, but Miss Tysoe was right – the place was a tip.

Books were everywhere. Some embroidery had been started and then left on the sofa. Magazines were piled on tables. On a pair of slippers which had been left in front of the TV lay a beautiful white cat – he was the only tidy thing in the place.

'Cool cat,' I said.

'Charlie.' Miss Tysoe leant down to stroke the cat which looked up at her through narrowed eyes. 'He's my prince.'

Miss Tysoe seemed to have got used to the idea of a football star appearing in her back garden one Sunday afternoon. Over tea, we talked about the game. I told her some of the things that had been said in the dressing room.

'Do you always celebrate like that?' she asked at one point.

'Like what?'

'Kissing someone in the crowd.'

For a moment, I wanted to point out that it had been she who had grabbed me, but I decided to be polite. 'We're very emotional where I come from,' I said.

Uh-oh. As I spoke these words, I saw this great trap opening in front of me. One little lie was going to need a bigger lie to cover it up which would then have to be supported by a total whopper. From there, it was bye-bye reality.

'And where do you come from?'

I swallowed. 'Blah . . . Blahvia.'

'Blahvia?'

'It's a very small country. It used to be part of Russia.' I shook my head. 'We have loads of problems

181

there. Revolutions. Wars. Earthquakes. I don't like to talk about it, to tell the truth.'

'I'm sorry. What team did you play for there?'

Good question. 'Dynamo Blahvia. It's the only team in Blahvia.'

Miss Tysoe frowned. 'So who did you play against?'

I sipped my tea slowly, giving myself time to think. 'That's why I left Blahvia. We just played five-a-sides and friendlies. It was lame.'

'So how did you end up at City?'

By now I was regretting having started this conversation but there was no turning back. 'You know Joe Smith, the youth team manager? He was on holiday in Blahvia. He saw me playing. Signed me up.'

'Unbelievable.'

'What? Oh yeah, I suppose it is a bit unbelievable.' I smiled. 'What about you?'

To my relief, Miss Tysoe sat back in her chair and began to talk about school – about our class, the pressures, how she didn't get on with some of the other teachers. To tell the truth, it was really interesting. Until then, I had seen her as the person who came into class, who was usually in a good mood, sometimes a bit grumpy. I hadn't ever thought of all the problems and worries she had when she wasn't with us. To hear her talk, teaching was the easy bit. 'I've got all that marking to do by tomorrow.' She nodded in the direction of a pile of exercise books on a table in the corner.

'Tough break,' I said.

'So.' She looked back at me. 'Why don't you tell me what this is all about?'

It was the moment of truth. Yet – maybe because truth and me had parted company some time ago – I suddenly found it hard just to spill it all out, to tell her that there never was a Blahvia, let alone a Dynamo Blahvia, that there was only a boy called Stanley who became Lazlo and now wanted to be Stanley again.

'I'm trying to get away from people.'

'What kind of people?'

'Anyone who knows Lazlo.'

'But everyone knows Lazlo.'

'Exactly. I remembered you from the match and . . .' I thought hard. Of all the teachers I had ever known, Miss Tysoe was the best at seeing through a story. 'So I checked with the box office. They knew who you were from your season ticket.'

'But why me?'

'You seemed like someone I could trust. Someone who wouldn't ask too many questions.'

'So you want a hideaway? For how long?'

'Just until tomorrow. I need to work some things out.'

Miss Tysoe was shaking her head. 'I don't think so,' she said. 'I don't know you. I'm alone . . .' For a moment, she seemed embarrassed. 'Most of the time, at least. Anyway, I've got to do my marking.'

It occurred to me that I could tell her my big secret a bit later. 'Just a couple of hours then?' I spoke quietly.

She stood up. 'I'm going to do some work. You can watch some television, if you have it on quietly. Right?'

'Yeah. Thanks, Miss Tysoe.'

'Gemma.'

'Thanks, Gemma.'

Maybe it was my heavy night, or my early start, or the stress of lying to Miss Tysoe. Perhaps it was the terrible things that being Lazlo was doing to my brain cells. Whatever the reason, I was suddenly feeling sleepy again. One moment I was watching some sappy TV programme about antiques, and thinking it was the sort of thing Mum liked to watch on a Sunday afternoon, and missing home, the next I was lying on the sofa, alone in the room.

It was getting dark now. From down the corridor, I could hear the sounds of a bath running. Miss Tysoe seemed to have put the room in order. Instead of exercise books on the corner table, there were knives and forks and wine glasses. Two places had been laid. In the middle of the table was a candle.

I sat up slowly, wondering what I should do. Sneak out while there was still time? Tell Miss Tysoe the truth before the situation became even more embarrassing?

Then I had the biggest shock of my life. I heard my name coming from the television.

' . . . Stanley Peterson, the boy who has been missing since yesterday's football match between City and Liverpool.'

It was the early evening news and the man reading it had that gloomy, I'm-really-sorry-I-have-to-tell-you-this look that newspeople put on when something terrible has happened, like a plane crash.

I leapt across the room to turn the volume lower, so that Miss Tysoe wouldn't hear.

'The eleven-year-old was thought to have met his father after the game . . .' My last photograph in the world, an embarrassingly nerdish school portrait of me taken last year, flashed on to the screen. 'But police were alerted to his disappearance early this morning. Anyone who has news of Stanley's whereabouts or who believes they saw him before, during or after yesterday's game is asked to contact police on this number . . .'

I thought of Mum and how worried she must be. Without a moment's hesitation, I grabbed the telephone which was by the sofa and dialled while the number was on the screen.

'Incident desk.' A woman's voice answered after the first ring.

'It's about Stanley Peterson,' I murmured into the handset, keeping an eye on the bathroom door.

'Have you seen him?'

'Yes. No. I mean—'

'Whereabouts did you see him?'

'He's safe. Tell his parents he'll be home tomorrow.'

'Your name, please, sir?' The woman's voice suggested that this wasn't the first nuisance call she had received today.

'It's Lazlo,' I said.

'Oh yeah? We're dealing with a child's life and you're having a laugh.'

'But—'

'I should warn you that wasting police time is a criminal offence and that we can trace this call.'

I put down the receiver slowly. On the screen, there were pictures of a hospital, then two old people walking down a corridor, then a demonstration outside a factory. News. Life. People. For a moment, I considered ringing Mum myself but what could I say? The sound of a deep-voiced foreigner who knew where her son was wouldn't be exactly reassuring. Maybe if Miss Tysoe—

'Any news?'

The voice came from behind me. I shook my head. 'Not really.' I turned away from the TV. 'Nothing int . . . int . . .'

It was Miss Tysoe standing in the middle of the room, yet it wasn't. She was wearing this short skirt and loose purple silk shirt. There was some sort of pale lipstick on her lips. She had done something weird to her hair. She smelt like a hairdressing salon.

'Interesting?' She smiled. I had seen Miss Tysoe smile lots of times but this was different. It was as if she and I were sharing a secret that no one else in the world knew. Warm, friendly, almost . . . romantic?

And suddenly I started to worry.

# CHAPTER 26

## 'You've changed . . .'

. . . I said.

'It's not every day I have a celebrity for dinner.' Miss Tysoe sort of ambled past me to the kitchen. 'Does the great Lazlo like pasta?'

'You bet,' I said. 'He really likes pasta.'

'If you want to freshen up, the bathroom's down the corridor,' she called out from the kitchen. 'I've left out some shaving things.'

'Shaving things?'

'I had this friend who used to stay. He left his razor.'

'Right, great. Back of the net.'

I wandered down the corridor, into the bathroom. Staring into the mirror, I was shocked by the way I looked.

There were rings under my eyes. The hair on my

head was sticking out like a scarecrow's. The dark stubble on my chin was now so long that it was almost a beard. I didn't look like a footballer any more. I looked like a terrorist.

I picked up the razor from a shelf under the mirror. A friend, eh? Miss Tysoe was one of those teachers who avoided talking about her private life but somehow I had never thought of her having a boyfriend. She didn't seem the type.

There was a can of shaving cream next to the razor. I took off the top and pressed the lever. It squirted a snowball of foam into my hand. I dabbed it on my chin until I had a big white beard. I picked up the razor and scraped my chin with it.

*Aagghh!* Agony. I had always thought razors were meant to cut hairs, not pull them out by the roots. Was this what men went through every morning? I remembered how Dad often used to be in a really bad mood at breakfast. Now I understood why.

I squirted some more shaving cream in the general direction of my face in a pathetic effort to kill the pain but most of it seemed to go into my hair. I scraped again. A small drop of blood appeared on my cheek. Taking a deep breath, I attacked my face once more – after all, it wouldn't exactly look good if Lazlo couldn't stand the pain of a bit of shaving. Five long minutes later, my chin was slightly smoother but there was blood and foam everywhere – I looked like a Santa Claus who had just been mugged.

'Blimey, what happened to you?' When I emerged from the bathroom, Miss Tysoe was lighting the candles on the table.

'Bit of a heavy beard,' I said.

Miss Tysoe laughed. 'The razor was probably blunt. It hasn't been used for a while.' She suddenly looked thoughtful. 'No, not for quite a while now.'

Pulling herself together, she was back to her normal, brisk self. 'Let's eat,' she said.

My plan had seemed so simple. I'd wait for a moment in the evening when Miss Tysoe was relaxed. Then, very slowly and sensibly, I'd break the news of what had happened to me. City. Cybertelekinesis. The magic stud. How I had become trapped in Lazlo's body. The story on the news.

As a teacher, she was good in a crisis, Miss Tysoe – decisive and sympathetic at the same time. With her on my side, I'd go back to my mum and explain the truth about Lazlo. With her help, I would be all right.

It was just a question of choosing the right moment.

'How was the marking?' I asked.

She winced. 'Not exactly the way I like to spend my Sundays.'

'Any good work there?' I asked, unable to hide my curiosity.

'They're not bad kids. I asked them to take a fairy

story and put it in a modern setting. Some of the answers were brilliant.'

'Like for instance?'

'The best one was the story of Little Red Riding Hood set in a space station. The granny was an astronaut and the wolf ended up getting sent to Mars.' She shook her head. 'He's got such a weird imagination, that Dominic.'

'Dominic!' I couldn't hide my surprise. 'I mean . . . Dominic? That's a nice name.'

Miss Tysoe was looking at me strangely. 'What were you like at school, Lazlo?'

'Not bad. My teacher used to get a bit stressed because everything I did ended up being about football.'

'Yes, we have a boy like that. More salad?'

*And*, I wanted to say. *And?* I waited for a moment but Miss Tysoe said nothing. 'What's his name?' I asked casually.

'Stanley,' she smiled vaguely. 'Nice boy. Bit of a dreamer. I'll get the fettuccine.'

Nice? Dreamer? Gee, thanks a bunch, Miss Tysoe.

She returned with a bowl of pasta. 'Want to pour the wine?' she asked.

Despite the disappointing news that I was no more than just a nice boy to Miss Tysoe, it was a good evening. She had a way of doing pasta so that it wasn't as if it had been cooked in the glue which my mother seemed to use. The white wine relaxed me, seemed to ease my worries about what my

191

parents were thinking. I liked wine. When I returned to being Stanley, that would be one part of life as Lazlo that I would miss.

Or, rather, *if* I ever returned to being Stanley.

Time seemed to speed by. Miss Tysoe talked about her life at school. I kept delaying the moment when I'd break the news that I was not Lazlo, but her nice boy in disguise.

We finished eating. I sat back in my chair, took a deep breath. 'There's something I've got to tell you,' I said.

'Me too.' She smiled and took another sip of wine.

'Right, but—'

'Can I go first?'

I shrugged.

'I just wanted to thank you, Lazlo – thank you for everything. For yesterday at the City Stadium. For tonight and . . .' She glanced down at her food, then looked into my eyes. 'And for that kiss.'

Gulp. Lemme outta here.

'Kiss? It was nothing. Honestly.'

'It was something.' Miss Tysoe was giving a moody look that made me want to hide under the table.

'Yeah, maybe it was something,' I said as politely as I could manage. 'But . . . I just don't want you to say anything we both might regret.'

'Why should I—?'

'Just believe me on this. You really might regret it.'

'All I was going to say is that I've got a boyfriend.'

'Phew,' I said.

'What?'

'I mean, few . . . few people would guess that you had a boyfriend.'

'His name is Barry. He works in Nottingham. We went out together until February this year. I had this idea that we were seeing too much of each other. Too much too soon. You know?'

'Right.'

'So when his firm moved him to Nottingham, it seemed a good time to make a break. Give us each a little space. That was it, finito. Until the kiss.'

'Our kiss?'

Miss Tysoe nodded. 'Barry and I used to go to City games together. He recognized me on *Match of the Day*. He telephoned me last night. We're getting back together. Thanks to Lazlo.'

'Glad to be of help.'

'I've suddenly realized that I just want to be with Barry. I rang him today. I'm going up to Nottingham next weekend.'

'Does that mean you'll be supporting Forest?'

'Not unless Lazlo gets transferred to them.'

'No way.'

'So that was what I wanted to tell you.' She smiled. 'If it hadn't been for you, none of that would have happened.' She sat back in her chair. 'Your turn now.'

'For what?'

'You said there was something you had to tell me. Something important.'

'Oh yeah, right.' What could I do? Tell her that she had just confessed her big, romantic secret to Stanley Peterson from school? My brilliant plan lay in pieces around my feet. 'I wanted to thank you too.'

'That was it?'

'Yes. Um, thanks very much.'

'Oh, Lazlo.' She squeezed my hand. 'I think I know what you were going to say.'

'You don't.' To my horror, I realized that Miss Tysoe was going all misty-eyed again. 'I promise. You really don't know what I was going to say.'

'I understand.' She held my hand even more tightly. 'But it never would have worked out between us. I mean, you're not in my class, are you?'

'I am. I mean − in a way.'

'We're different, Lazlo.

I managed to extricate my hand. 'So is there any chance of sleeping on your sofa? I'll be off in the morning.'

For a moment, she seemed uncertain but then nodded. 'Of course.'

We both stood up, a bit embarrassed by the way the conversation had gone. In that moment of hesitation, I became aware of a dodgy, puckering-up sort of movement from Miss Tysoe. She took a step forward but this time, unlike at the City Stadium, I was ready for the snog-attack.

I twitched my right hand and swept a wine glass from the table. As it crashed to the floor, I ducked down, leaving her kissing the air.

'Sorry, Miss Tysoe.' I began to pick up the pieces.

She walked briskly to the door, once again her old self. 'I'll fetch you a blanket,' she said.

# CHAPTER 27

## My teacher was looking down at me . . .

. . . shaking my shoulder.

'Wake up, Lazlo. I'm off in ten minutes,' she said, walking briskly to the kitchen. 'You'll have to leave, too. I've put on a pot of coffee.'

I sat up and watched her for a moment as she cleared the dinner dishes from the table and put them in the sink. Last night's misty romantic scene suddenly seemed like a distant memory. This was the Miss Tysoe I knew.

'I wanted to ask you a favour,' she was saying.

'Yeah?'

'It's probably not possible but I was wondering if you could present the prizes at a big cup match at our school on Tuesday.'

I winced. 'On Tuesday? I don't know who I'll

be on— I mean, I don't know where I'll be on Tuesday.'

Miss Tysoe stood in the centre of the room, her hands on her hips, giving me the sort of look she normally reserves for someone who hasn't done his homework.

'Typical celebrity,' she said. 'You kiss him, give him dinner, let him sleep on your couch – and he won't even give you half an hour of his time.'

'It's complicated.'

She was giving me that look again.

'All right, I'll try to be there.'

'Try?'

'And, if I can't be there, I'll get someone else from City.'

'It's at St Vincent Primary in St Vincent Lane.'

'I know . . . I know the way to St Vincent Lane. I've visited it a few times.'

Miss Tysoe was putting our exercise books in her briefcase. 'Knock back that coffee, Lazlo. I'm late.'

I stood up slowly. I'm not good in the morning, and nor was Lazlo. And that headache was back again. 'I feel terrible,' I said.

'Bit of fresh air, you'll soon be yourself again.'

'I really hope so,' I said, thinking of the day ahead of me.

The first problem was going to be getting home without being spotted by fans. I caught a glimpse of myself in a wall mirror. I looked rough, Steve

Malcolm's suit was crumpled and grey – but I was still Lazlo.

I took a gulp of coffee. It was gross. 'How am I going to get out of here without being recognized?'

'Car? Taxi? Minicab? Honestly, you superstars are so used to people arranging things, you've forgotten how the rest of us live our lives.'

'Not really.'

For the briefest moment, I thought of calling on Rafiq again, but even he might object to being called out for an unpaid ride which would take me five minutes on foot.

Miss Tysoe was standing in front of me. She had a pair of purple-rimmed dark glasses in her hand. 'Would these help?' she asked.

'Cool,' I said, putting them on.

'Not exactly,' said Miss Tysoe, laughing.

I looked at myself and groaned. 'I look like the Thing from Planet Dork. I'll take them. How can I get them back to you?'

Miss Tysoe had picked up her briefcase and was making her way to the front door. 'Tuesday,' she said firmly. 'Bring them then.'

'Right.'

She looked up at me as she pushed her bike out of the hall and opened the door. 'I wish I could think of who you remind me of,' she said.

'Someone nice, I hope.' I smiled at her, wondering when I would see her next, and how, praying to myself that, the next time we met, I'd be looking up at her, not down.

She held out a hand. 'I'll say goodbye here,' she said. 'I don't want to hang around on the doorstep, giving the neighbours something to gossip about.' She held out a hand. 'Goodbye, Lazlo.'

I shook her hand. 'Bye, Miss Tysoe.'

'Gemma.' She laughed. 'You sound just like one of my . . .' Suddenly she frowned. 'Yes, *that's* who you remind me of.

'See you, Gemma.'

I walked off quickly, head down, not looking back.

'I'll see you tomorrow,' she called after me. 'St Vincent Primary. Two o'clock.'

I raised a hand, one thumb up. I'd see her. Somehow.


Two days ago, I was the big hero. Now as I shuffled along, head down, in a sad crumpled suit, wearing Miss Tysoe's purple dark glasses, I felt like the local weirdo. No one paid me any attention. You have a certain walk if you're a celebrity, a certain look. Somewhere along the line I had lost it. I didn't feel famous. I didn't want to be famous. I just wanted to be Stanley Peterson again.

I thought of Callan and Angie and all my friends on their way to school. They were probably among the children who passed me by, chattering and swinging their satchels, but I wasn't going to risk looking up. I watched my feet, Lazlo's fabulous goal-scoring feet. One in front of the other, down the High Street, into our road, going home. At last.

It was quiet. For a moment, I had worried that there would be police at my house, or journalists, but if anything it seemed sleepier than usual, as if the whole street was in mourning for the lost boy of number 17.

I walked up my path and rang the bell by my front door. There was movement through the glass.

'Who is it?'

The voice from the far side of the door surprised me. It wasn't a voice that was often heard round these parts. It belonged to my dad. I swallowed hard. 'It's me,' I said. My low gravelly voice sounded cracked and odd, even to me.

Pause.

'And who's you?'

There was nothing for it. 'My name's Lazlo. I'm from the City Football Club.'

The door half-opened. Dad looked terrible, red-eyed and unshaven. He seemed to have aged about ten years. 'Lazlo? The footballer?'

'Right.'

'What do you want? What are you doing here?'

'Could I come in?'

Dad made no move. 'Look, if it's the club that's sent you round to say you're sorry about Stanley, that's very kind but—'

'It's not. It's . . . it's about Stanley.'

'You've got news?'

'Yes.'

Dad stepped back to let me in. 'The sitting room's through there and to the right.'

I stepped into the hall, into the happy, familiar smell of home.

'Sue,' he called up the stairs. 'Could you come down a minute?'

I went into the sitting room and stood in front of the fireplace. The room was unusually tidy. It ached with the absence of Stanley. Dad stood at the door. Then Mum was beside him. She was still in her dressing gown and her eyes were swollen. Dad sort of supported her, one hand under her elbow as if she was a patient in hospital. I hadn't seen them standing together, touching, for years.

'This is Lazlo.' Dad spoke softly. 'He plays for City. He says he's got some news for us.'

'News?' Her voice was a whisper of despair. 'What news?'

'It's . . .' Suddenly I didn't know where to start.

'Come on, Mr Lazlo,' said Dad. 'We're not in the mood for polite conversation. Just tell us what you have to say and leave us alone.'

And suddenly I couldn't hold it in any more. I was shaking with sobs, my face wet with tears.

They both looked at me, amazed.

'What is this?' said Dad.

Eventually I managed to speak. 'Mum, Dad,' I said. 'It's me.'

# CHAPTER 28

## They seemed to move closer . . .

. . . to one another, as if I was some kind of dangerous psycho. Mum was the first to speak.

'Is this some kind of joke?' she asked.

I wiped my face on the jacket of my suit. 'Please sit down,' I said. 'I'll try to explain.'

To my surprise, they moved forward obediently and sat down together on the sofa, staring suspiciously at me all the while. 'If this is some kind of press trick, I'm calling the police.'

'It's not.' I took a deep breath. 'I'm Stanley,' I said.

My father balled his fist with rage. 'He's a nutter,' he said, half out of his seat, but Mum held him back, her eyes fixed on mine.

'It was the computer,' I whispered. 'It was cyber-telekinesis.'

'Right, out – now!' snapped my father.

'No.' My mother shook her head like someone caught up in a nightmare. 'It can't be true.'

I stood up, took off my jacket. I rolled up my sleeve carefully, slowly.

My mother screamed when she saw it.

There, against the dark skin of Lazlo's muscular arm was a small, square sticking plaster. On it was the face of Popeye.

I pulled my sleeve down and returned to my chair. 'Can I tell you what happened?'

Parents are weird. You'd think that discovering your son has been turned into a dark, hairy bloke with a funny accent would be just as bad as simply losing him but, once Mum and Dad had been convinced that Lazlo was Stanley, they seemed to calm down. My father, I had to admit, wandered about the room, muttering to himself and swearing.

'I hate bloomin' computers,' he said.

'And I hate bloomin' football,' replied my mother.

We all looked at each other, remembering old rows, and probably for the first time for a while, there was laughter in the house.

'It's all very well,' said Dad. 'But if he's lost this bloomin' stud or whatever, how's he going to get back to being Stanley?'

The colour had returned to my mother's cheeks. She had the absent-minded professor look on her face from which I knew she was working out some ridiculously complicated formula in her head. 'Shush,' she said. 'I'm working.'

'Oh, hullo, here we go again,' Dad muttered. 'Just like old times.'

'Er, with one small difference,' I said.

'We've got to get experts in,' he said. 'There must be other people working in this area.'

Mum emerged briefly from her trance. 'Call up a computer helpline, you mean? Ask them if they could send someone round to turn a hulking great footballer back into an eleven-year-old boy? Get real, darling.'

'If it wasn't for your damned research, we wouldn't have had all this trouble.'

'Yeah,' I said, 'and City would have been relegated.'

'Maybe not.' Dad shrugged. 'I reckon Martin Sturgess would have scored anyway.'

'What? I set him up, Dad.'

'Shut up about football!' Mum screamed at the top of her voice.

For a few seconds, there was silence in the room.

'We can't tell anyone about this.' She spoke more quietly. 'Once we get the cyber crew involved, anything could happen. We'd probably lose Lazlo and get a white mouse instead.'

'Mum, please don't make jokes like that.'

She looked at me, unsmiling. 'Who said it was a joke?' She stood up. 'Come with me, Stanley,' she said briskly. 'I think I know what to do.' Dad stood up too but Mum shook her head. 'I think you'd better stay downstairs.'

'Anything you say, Dr Frankenstein,' said Dad.

'What happened to the Dweeble?'

I was sitting on a chair in Mum's study watching her fiddle around with the computer. 'He's downstairs,' she said absent-mindedly. 'Didn't you notice him?'

'I mean, that's not the Dweeble. That's Dad. You're talking to him – treating him like a human. He's managing to stay in one place without running away after about ten seconds. You're both acting like . . . I dunno, parents.'

Mum kept her eyes on the screen, but I could tell she was embarrassed. 'He came round yesterday as soon as he heard you were missing. We needed to deal with the police, the press. I was in a pretty bad way thanks to you and your bloomin' Lazlo. He . . . behaved well. He stayed the evening, then the night. End of story. Now . . .' She pushed back her chair and turned to me. I had quite a few more questions to ask about her and Dad but for some reason her mind was on getting her son back. 'While you've been yakking away, I've been looking through the CBTK database.'

'CBTK?'

'Cybertelekinesis.' Mum was gathering speed now, leaving the realm of normal human conversation for the weird and wacky world of computer science. 'Stanley, you're going to have to wise up if we're going to manage this thing.'

'I'm not Stanley. I'm still Lazlo.'

'What I'm trying to tell you is that you became Lazlo as a result of an unusually strong power surge from your brain . . .'

'Right.'

'It was your will to save your football team that activated an abnormally high alpha wave current from the cerebral cortex. To reverse the process, you need to really want to be Stanley Peterson again.'

'That's no problem. I want to be me more than anything else in the world.'

'The second problem is that the computer doesn't recognize your UIP – that's Unique Individuation Profile.'

'Er, translation.'

'Lazlo existed as a recognized entity within cyberspace. So what you did was transfer him from virtuality into flesh and blood.'

'Ah. I think I'm beginning to see the problem.'

'The computer's never heard of Stanley Peterson. I could spend all day trying to create a computer profile of you but it wouldn't be you.

'Give us another six inches' height, Mum,' I said gloomily. 'I was fed up with being a titch.'

But she didn't laugh.

'The way I brought up Lazlo was by introducing the *TargetMan* disk,' I said. 'Maybe we could work out some kind of Stanley disk.'

'Your geography project.' My mother leapt up and went to a side table where there was a rack of disks.

'Eh? That was all about pedestrianizing streets in an average market town.'

She had found the disk and slipped it into the computer. 'The UIP is often established automatically. Your personality comes through in the writing, the layout — we don't know how it works but it does.' She was standing in front of the computer. 'I think we might be in business,' she said, beckoning me to the chair in front of the computer.

I sat down and stared at the screen. It read:

UIP IDENTITY UNKNOWN

The electrodes hairnet was on the table in front of me. Mum put it carefully on my head. Once again I felt the cool metal lobes against my temple. Mum was tapping the keyboard.

STANLEY PETERSON?

'Mum, I'm worried about that geography project. I only got a C for it.'

'Concentrate, Stanley.'

'I don't want to come back as a pedestrianized High Street.'

IDENTITY UNKNOWN

Mum tapped again. For the first time I noticed that little droplets of sweat had formed on her top lip.

STANLEY PETERSON?

A peculiar sense of fear had begun to grip my heart. I had always assumed that, when she wanted to do something on a computer, Mum could do it. But there was something about the way she kept repeating the same command, the frantic stabbing movements of her fingers on the keyboard, which told me that something was wrong. Mum was no longer in control.

STANLEY PETERSON?

IDENTITY UNKNOWN

STANLEY PETERSON?

IDENTITY UNKNOWN

STANLEY PETERSON?

IDENTITY UNKNOWN

'Why don't you lose the question mark? Give it a command. It's almost as if you're asking the computer to do you a favour.'

'One more,' Mum whispered. 'Don't talk. Con-

centrate with all your mind on being Stanley.' She
tapped the keyboard.

STANLEY PETERSON

I squeezed my eyes shut. I thought of waking up in
my bed on a Saturday morning when City were due
to play at home. I thought of the smell of breakfast.
I thought of playing football with Callan and
Angie. I thought of Mum and Dad, standing
together in the sitting room, as if they had never
been apart. I thought of me in my room, alone,
Stanley. I opened my eyes.

IDENTITY UNKNOWN

I took off the headset and sat back in my chair.
'Sorry, Mum,' I said quietly. 'It was easy when I was
willing Lazlo into life. I knew what I wanted — a
footballing superhero to save City from relegation.
But wanting to be Stanley . . .' I shrugged. 'I am
Stanley. It's difficult to want to be what you think
you are already.'

Mum was looking at me in an odd way, excited
yet fearful. I knew her well enough to know that
she had had an idea, yet something told me it was
unlikely to be entirely good news.

'There's only one escape,' she whispered. 'And it's
very risky.'

'Yeah, back of the net. Let's go for it. Er, how d'you mean risky?'

'Lazlo must die,' she said.

When I found words, they weren't the words I was feeling.

'That's nice,' I said. 'My own mum, too.'

She laid a hand on mine and looked into my eyes. 'We're never going to get you back to Stanley by brainpower alone. But if we take Lazlo away – give him a negative identity – we should be left with what was here before.'

'Me.'

'You.'

'What happens if I get a negative identity, too?'

'I don't think it will happen. The essence of Lazlo is Stanley. We're just eliminating the outer shell.'

'Yeah, great, Mum. And maybe eliminating this outer shell will destroy what's underneath.'

'Nothing's a hundred per cent certain in science. But I don't think we've got a choice. Unless you want to stay Lazlo and see what happens.'

I thought of Steve Malcolm, of Terry Mills, of Julie. I remembered how nobody treated me as normal, how, at every moment, decisions crowded in on me. Life as Lazlo was all right on the pitch, but the rest of it was nothing but stress and trouble. 'No way,' I said. 'But what would happen to Lazlo?' I pinched my powerful right thigh. 'He – I – exists.'

210

'We'd wipe the whole program. He'd disappear into the cybervoid. He'd be a blank.'

'He was the best striker City ever had.'

Mum smiled. 'He'll still be in the record books. People will say, "Whatever happened to Lazlo?" And only you, me and Dad will know the truth.'

'He was a nice bloke, Lazlo.'

'He was you. And you'll still be around.' Mum was looking through the computer disks. She found *TargetMan* and slipped it into the computer.

'You hope.'

'Yes. I hope.' She put the hairnet on me again. 'Wait here a minute.'

I heard her going downstairs. There were raised voices from the sitting room, followed by a long period of silence, then a few murmured phrases. Footsteps on the stairs. Mum and Dad entered the study.

My father put his hand on my shoulder. 'Byebye, Lazlo, eh?'

'Yeah.' I noticed his eyes were damp.

'You all right about it?'

I nodded. 'If you can't trust your mother, who can you?'

Dad looked as if he was about to make a joke but then had thought better of it. 'Good lad,' he said.

'You're not losing Lazlo.' Mum stepped forward and turned the keyboard towards her. 'You're getting back Stanley.'

On the screen, the words appeared:

Mum tapped a key. Suddenly I was staring at my face in the screen. It was exactly how it was when I had first become Lazlo.

She tapped again.

LAZLO PROGRAM ERASE?

Tap.

WARNING: IF THIS PROGRAM IS ERASED, UIP IDENTITY WILL BE DESTROYED. CANCEL COMMAND?

Tap.

UIP IDENTITY LAZLO: CONFIRM COMMAND

My mother hesitated. 'Ready, love?' she whispered.

I looked round at my mother, at my father whose arm was round her waist. She kissed me lightly on the head. Dad squeezed my shoulder.

'Just relax, Stanley.' Mum touched Dad gently on the arm. 'Stand back,' she said.

Her finger hesitated over the keyboard. She took a deep breath and . . .

# CHAPTER 29

## I was on fire . . .

. . . In a split second, a searing flash of pain in the
pit of my stomach spread outwards, down my arms
and legs, up my throat, into my skull until the whole
of me was a thundering, aching fireball. There were
voices, screams, a crash, but they were a million
miles away in another universe. I was hurtling
through time, blazing in dazzling pain, exploding
outwards like a star in space, bright at first, then
flickering, fading darker and darker until there was
nothing to me but a great silent blackness that
descended on me, burying me, stifling me, one tiny
spark remaining in front of my eyes, flaring moment-
arily. Then, in a little pop, that too was gone and
silence was everywhere.

# CHAPTER 30

## There was a light . . .

. . . but it wasn't expanding or exploding. It wasn't dazzling me. It had a lampshade.

I was in my bed, in my room. Slowly, hardly daring to look, I raised my hand. It was Stanley's hand. I touched my chin. It was smooth. I felt my body and started laughing. I was me again.

I got out of bed. I was in my pyjamas now. My dressing gown was lying across the bed, my slippers were neatly under my chair. I put them on. It felt great to be normal.

I must have walked downstairs quietly because, when I walked into the sitting room, Mum and Dad looked at me as if an angel had just appeared in their room.

Then all hell broke loose. If someone had looked through our window at that moment, they would have thought the Peterson family was having this huge wrestling match. After about five minutes, we sorted ourselves out. I sat between them on the sofa.

'What happened to me?' I asked.

'It was horrible.' Mum shook her head. 'One moment you were Lazlo, sitting in front of the computer. The next, you seemed to be breaking up like an image on a faulty TV screen. You faded and faded until there was nothing but a sort of grey haze. All I could hear was your father's voice. "Where's Stanley?" he was saying. "Where's he gone?" '

Dad closed his eyes at the memory. 'I thought we'd lost you,' he whispered.

'Then there was this noise behind us. A sort of gasp, like someone trying to catch his breath after a long dive under water. And there you were, curled up on the floor, naked – as if you had just been reborn.'

'Ugh, embarrassing,' I said. 'I'm glad no one else was there.'

'We were a bit worried because you seemed in a sort of trance,' said Mum. 'But you didn't have a temperature so we thought we'd let you sleep it off.'

'The police took a bit of convincing,' said Dad. 'but I managed to persuade them you had stayed at a friend's without telling us.'

My mother put an arm around me. 'How are you feeling now?'

'A bit woozy but fine.'

'You'll be all right for school tomorrow, then?' asked Dad.

'No problem.' A distant memory nagged at me, as if I had managed to forget something important.

'We might come down and watch the Cup game,' said Dad.

'Match?' Suddenly I remembered. I had promised Miss Tysoe that Lazlo would present the cup.

The late Lazlo. Lazlo the blank.

'Who on earth gave you these?' On a table nearby were a few mementoes of my life as Lazlo. With obvious distaste, Mum was holding Miss Tysoe's purple dark glasses.

'Just a friend.'

'A friend?' asked Dad suspiciously.

'And who's Terry Mills?' Mum was looking at Lazlo's two calling cards.

'He was just someone I met.'

'Well, I'm going to cook us some supper.' My mother stood up. 'A family meal.'

'First she agrees to watch a football match at school. Then she's cooking supper. What's happening?' said Dad.

'Watch it, you,' said Mum, but there was a smile on her face.

Something was on Dad's mind. He seemed embarrassed. It took all of two minutes as we listened to the sounds from the kitchen for the problem to emerge.

216

'There was one other thing, Stanley,' he said in his best I'm-a-responsible-father voice. Glancing towards the door to check that Mum was not about to enter, he reached under the cushion of the sofa. Hidden there was a copy of that day's *Daily Star*. 'While you were asleep, I went to the shops. I happened to notice this newspaper.' He passed it to me.

It was a Lazlo story, of course. A Lazlo story with a difference. I WAS DUMPED BY LOVE-RAT LAZLO! read the headline. Underneath, in smaller letters, was written: *'He was a lion on the pitch – but a tiger back at my place,' reveals model Julie Simpkins.*

I gulped. 'Eh?'

Beside the story were two pictures – one of Lazlo scoring his second goal against Liverpool, the other of my old friend Julie wearing even less than she was at the nightclub last Saturday.

I turned to an inside page. There was another shot of me and Julie getting into her car. Beside it was the note I had left her – THANK YOU VERY MUCH FOR HAVING ME, LOVE LAZLO – with a caption reading, *Lazza reveals his famous sense of humour in a cruel goodbye note to gorgeous Julie.*

'You don't have to read it all,' said Dad. 'After all, you were there, weren't you?'

I smiled. So Julie had made a bit of pocket money for herself by making up a story about Lazlo, the love-rat, and selling it to a newspaper. 'Yeah, I was there.'

Dad shifted uncomfortably. 'I think we should have a talk about this.'

'Talk?'

'I mean, did you . . .? You and this Julie, were you . . .?'

There would be a time to tell him the truth about the love-rat and Julie but somehow it didn't seem the moment. I remembered a phrase I had read somewhere. 'We were just good friends,' I said.

My father seemed satisfied by this reply. 'I'm throwing this away, Stanley,' he muttered. 'Your mother's had enough shocks for one day.'

'Back of the net, Dad.' I picked up the card with Steve Malcolm's home number on it. 'Could I make a telephone call from upstairs?'

'You're not calling that Julie, I hope.'

I smiled. 'Julie who, Dad?'

'Steve Malcolm speaking. Who is this?'

'You don't need to know my name. Lazlo asked me to call you.'

'You're that kid, right? The one who came to my house.'

'Never mind that. The message from Lazlo is that he's decided he wants to sign up with the agent you suggested.'

'Yeah?'

'He's prepared to go on the transfer market. Although obviously he'd prefer to stay at City.'

'Yeah, yeah. So where's he gone to now?'

'He's had to go into hiding. Personal problems.'

'Tell him I'll be at the ground tomorrow afternoon. We'll sign the papers then.'

'Er, no. He'll be there tomorrow evening if you agree to present the cup at the senior match between St Vincent Primary and Chester Gardens tomorrow afternoon.'

'Eh? A schoolkids' match? Are you having a laugh?'

'That's the deal. If you want to see Lazlo again, you have to be at the St Vincent sports ground, St Vincent Road, tomorrow afternoon.'

'I don't believe this. I'll be glad to see the back of that . . . that foreigner.'

'Two-thirty, St Vincent's,' I said. 'Agreed?'

'Maybe. But don't hold your breath.'

# CHAPTER 31

## School was buzzing . . .

. . . but the excitement was not about the return of Stanley Peterson. Everyone was talking about the big game against Chester Gardens – and the guest celebrity who would be presenting the cup. On each of the noticeboards was the same proud announcement:

*Today. 2.30pm*
*St Vincent Primary XI*
*V.*
*Chester Gardens Primary XI*
*Special guest: City football star LAZLO*

'All the parents are coming to see him – it's going to be amazing,' Callan told me as we waited for the first lesson to start.

'Mine too,' I smiled. 'Even my mum.'

'You'll never guess who invited him.'

Not in a million years. 'Miss Boston?'

'Miss Tysoe. She's been going out with him.'

'Yeah?' I tried to sound casual. 'Didn't she have a boyfriend or something?'

I dropped my voice as Miss Tysoe entered the classroom. There was a new curiosity about her among the children and, as if she could sense this, she was walking with a certain self-confidence.

Angie leant across from the next door desk. 'He stayed the night with her,' she said in loud whisper. 'Someone saw him leave in the morning.'

As I groaned to myself, Miss Tysoe rapped the desk in front of her. 'Morning, everyone,' she said cheerfully. 'And welcome back, Stanley.' She gave her public, teacher's smile, so different from the last smile I had seen on her face. 'I might have known you'd manage to get back in time to see our famous visitor, Mr Lazlo.'

'Too right. I wouldn't have missed that for the world.'


The lesson was maths, my worst subject. It was perfect.

To tell the truth, a frightening thought had been nagging me more and more insistently since I had woken this morning – a worry that I could share with no one, not even my mother.

I had been to the magical land of Lazlo. I had

returned safely. But what had those two days spent in virtual reality done to my brain cells?

I spoke all right. My memory for names seemed to be OK. But the best way to test whether I was still thinking straight was to try a few sums. Long multiplication. Long division. If I could get my usual mark – around 45% was my average – then I'd know I was in as good a mental shape as I'd ever be.

There were ten sums, five of each. Ignoring the chatter around me, I concentrated on my work as I'd never done before.

After half an hour, Miss Tysoe asked Callan to collect the exercise books for marking that night. I couldn't wait that long. As Callan did his rounds, I walked up to her desk.

'Could you look at mine now, please, Miss Tysoe?'

She looked at me curiously. 'Are you all right, Stanley?' she asked. 'You seem very quiet today.'

'I'm fine, miss.'

She took the exercise book and reached for the red biro she uses for marking.

Tick. Tick. Cross. Tick. Cross. Tick. I began to breathe again. It wasn't brilliant but then a Stanley Peterson maths test was never going to be brilliant.

'Careless,' Miss Tysoe muttered, putting a cross beside the last sum. She counted the ticks. 'Seven out of ten. Not bad, Stanley. Not great, but not bad.'

The classroom door opened. In his usual brisk and unapologetic manner, the games master Mr

O'Reardon walked in and stood in front of Miss Tysoe's desk, his back to the class.

'Bit of a problem this afternoon, Gemma,' he said in a voice the children behind him couldn't hear. 'Jones has got tonsillitis. I need someone for the game this afternoon. There'll be a riot if I ask for volunteers, what with Lazlo coming and all.'

'What position does Jones play?'

'On the right of midfield.'

Miss Tysoe put a hand on my shoulder. 'You're a midfielder, aren't you, Stanley?'

I nodded.

O'Reardon shook his head dismissively.

'They're big lads, Chester Gardens.'

'So were Liverpool.' I spoke with quiet determination. 'Think what that little bloke Lazlo did for them.'

Mr O'Reardon looked down at me. 'But we're not Lazlo, are we?'

I looked him in the eye. 'No. We're Stanley, sir.'

He hesitated, then gave Miss Tysoe an unfriendly look. 'On your head be it, Gemma,' he said. 'Two o'clock. Sports ground. You're in.' He walked out, closing the door noisily behind him.

'Thanks, Miss Tysoe,' I said.

'Don't let me down,' she said.


*Peterson takes possession in midfield, he glances up, he turns and—*

Oooofff!

*Still looking a bit shaky, the little midfielder is waiting for the ball on the centre spot. Here it comes, he controls to—*

Crrrrunchhh!

*It's a great cross from the right wing and Peterson's sprinting forward to meet it at the back of the box, but so's a big defender—*

Bangggg!

The first half against Chester Gardens reminded me of what football's like in the real world when you don't happen to be someone who can make a football do anything, go anywhere that he wants.

There was the biggest crowd that had ever been seen at St Vincent – parents, children, journalists, passers-by had been waiting at the football pitch for the arrival of the great Lazlo. When it was Steve Malcolm who stepped out of the Jaguar with dark windows, there was a brief murmur of disappointment in the crowd but soon the excitement of having the one and only manager of City Football Club had seemed to make them forget all about Lazlo.

Steve Malcolm was famous. He appeared on television. His face was in the papers. It was enough.

Chester Gardens didn't exactly foul but, whenever I was around they used their strength to kick, push, lean and barge me around. After 45 minutes, I felt like the little ball in a pinball machine.

By the time the half-time whistle blew, there had only been a few goal chances at each end, none of which had been taken. A nil–all bore draw.

Mr O'Reardon marched on to the pitch for his version of a team talk. As he ranted and raved at us, I watched Steve Malcolm chatting and signing autographs, surrounded by his admirers. He was one of those people who actually seemed to change physically when he was recognized, as if other people's admiration somehow brought him to life. When I had talked to him at his house or seen him at the City Stadium, he had seemed an average sort of bloke, a bit edgy and sarcastic but, underneath it all, dead ordinary. Now he was a hero, a celebrity. He looked the part.

At one point, he looked up and noticed me staring at him. Still signing autographs – he probably did that little squiggle of the right hand in his sleep – he narrowed his eyes as if suddenly remembering where he had seen me before.

'As for you, Peterson . . .'

I turned my attention Mr O'Reardon, who was shaking his head wearily. 'I know you've been trying, very trying . . .' He grinned at the other boys to make sure they had understood his lame joke. 'But you need to gain a foot in height and put on two stone.'

'Yes, sir.'

'Run around a bit and make a nuisance of yourself for a bit. I'll bring on a substitute in ten minutes.'

I nodded.

The referee was standing on the centre spot.

Ignoring the aches and pains in my back and legs, I stood up. We took our positions for the second half.

It was Chester Gardens' kick-off and they had obviously decided to catch us cold during the opening moments of the second half. Their central midfielder hoofed the ball forward and wide to the left wing. Their players advanced up the pitch in a great battle-charge of determination. Even their goalkeeper ran to the edge of his area, screaming encouragement.

Run around a bit. Make a nuisance of yourself. I heard Mr O'Reardon's words, glanced towards the touchline where he would be standing – and found myself staring into the eyes of Steve Malcolm, following my every move.

Suddenly I was back at the City Stadium. I was Lazlo, under the eye of his manager, the living hope of thousands of fans whose dreams were resting on my shoulders.

I sensed where the game had been going wrong for me. I had been trying to beat players on the other team at their own game, rushing, pushing, using strength not skill, playing the version of Stanley Peterson that other people saw – too small, too slow, too eager to please. It was simple: to win, I needed to be me, just as Lazlo had been Lazlo.

There was a desperate scrimmage in our area. Caught up in the panic of the moment, even our two strikers had fallen back. Chester Gardens' defence pushed up. There was only one of our players still in midfield and he, the opposition players seemed to have decided, could safely be ignored.

It was me.

For about the tenth time in the last minute, the ball was centred into the St Vincent area. A head, or maybe the goalkeeper's fist, made contact with it. A defender scooped the ball away in a desperate bid to relieve the pressure on our goal. It soared high and hopeless towards the halfway line.

*Oh, and Peterson's there. He's found acres of space for himself, but the two defenders are closing on him. He takes the ball on the chest. He flicks it over the lunging body of a defender. There's no one with him but, I don't believe this, he's going to . . .*

The goalkeeper was way off his line. One defender was out of contention, the other was still ten yards away. Slowly the ball fell. I hit it. Hard. The sweet spot. There was only one place it could go.

An eerie silence descended on the ground. The crowd watched the ball's perfect trajectory, the goalkeeper, arms waving, running backwards like a crazed puppet, the other players standing unable to do anything, to change the fate which was Stanley Peterson's perfectly weighted lob.

Only one place. Before it hit the back of the net, I had turned, arms held high, fists clenched. Victorious.

They didn't like it. The Chester Gardens players screamed at the keeper, yelled at each other. What little pattern there had been to Chester Gardens' play disappeared now. Every time the ball came near me, they bundled me over, conceding one free kick after another. They were not good losers.

Which was fine by us. The more they swore, the better we played. I thought of Lazlo – how he positioned himself, laid the ball off, took the return. Once I was a superhero in my head, it was easy. Five minutes before time, I took the ball thirty yards from goal, dummied to the left, then sidefooted the ball into the path of Jodie McIntyre, one of our strikers. He took it into the area and buried it.

Easy. Final whistle. The Cup was ours. Applause as we lined up to shake the hand of our celebrity guest.

And one last small problem.

'Well done, son.'

I was last in line. Steve Malcolm shook my hand.

'Thank you, sir.'

'Lovely lob, mate.' He shook my hand, squeezing it a bit more tightly.

'A bit lucky,' I said.

Holding on to my hand, he pulled me closer to him, the sincere nice-guy smile on his face never wavering. 'Where is he?' He spoke with quiet threat.

'Who?' I tugged at my hand but he had a powerful grip.

'You know who. He'll be at the ground later, right? To sign the papers?' There was a hint of panic in the manager's voice. 'There's a bob or two in this for you, son.'

My right hand was agony but no way was I going to show him I was in pain. 'Lazlo's going home,' I murmured.

'Eh?'

I jerked my arm as hard as I could. It came free. 'Thank you very much, Mr Malcolm,' I said loudly. 'It was very nice meeting you.'

The smile was wavering now. The manager looked pale.

Miss Boston appeared beside him. 'Would you care for a spot of tea, Mr Malcolm? We have a reception for parents and children in the school hall.'

He looked at me once more. Slowly and decisively, I shook my head.

'Mr Malcolm?' The headteacher gestured vaguely in the direction of the hall.

He turned to her, his face now dark with anger. 'You must be joking, you silly old bat,' he muttered. Brushing aside requests for his autograph as he made his way across the pitch towards where his car was parked.

'What very uncouth behaviour,' said Miss Boston.

'He's been under a lot of strain recently,' I said.

I felt an arm around me.

'That was the first game of football I've ever enjoyed,' said Mum.

I looked behind her. Miss Tysoe stood with my

father. 'Lazlo would have been proud of that first goal,' she said.

There was an awkward silence as Mum and Dad tried to think of something to say.

'Who's Lazlo?' asked my mother, blushing slightly at the lie.

'You must have heard about him.' Miss Tysoe's eyes seemed to light up at the thought of her new friend. 'In the game on Saturday—'

'Maybe we should join the others in the hall,' said Dad quickly.

'I'll just go and get changed.'

As casually as I could manage, I walked down the corridor, then slipped into our classroom. My satchel was by my desk. The purple sunglasses were in the side pocket where I had left them. I put them on Miss Tysoe's desk.

Then I reached inside the drawer of her desk for a sheet of paper. I picked up her pen and wrote:

*Dear Gemma*

*I'm very sorry that I was unable to attend the match today like I promised I would. Unfortunately I was called away to somewhere else. I hope my friend Steve Malcolm was a good substitute.*

*Here are your glasses. Thank you for lending them to me.*

*I'm afraid I won't be playing for City next season because I have been called back home to Blahvia for reasons beyond my control.*

*I hope it works out with Barry. Please don't move away to Nottingham because I know the children in your class really like being taught by you.*

*I will always remember how you helped me when I was in trouble. Although you won't see me again as the Lazlo you knew, I'm sure we'll meet again in some way or another.*

*Yours sincerely*

*Lazlo*
*xxx*

*PS What that girl Julie wrote in the papers about me being a love-rat was all invented. I just thought I'd mention that.*

I folded the paper and placed it under the dark glasses on her desk.

# CHAPTER 32

## In the school hall . . .

. . . there were only a few people left. Near the stage, Mr O'Reardon was telling some parents, yet again, how his tactical switch at half-time, pushing the lad Peterson forward, had swung the game in our favour. Miss Boston was standing at the door, wearing the expression of someone who had seen and talked about quite enough football for one day. A couple of minutes ago, Miss Tysoe had said her goodbyes and slipped away.

'Shall we go?' Dad smiled at Mum and me and, for the merest fraction of time, that 'we' hung in the air, like a challenge.

'Why not?' said Mum.

'I'll fetch my kit,' I said.

I walked quickly to the changing room, and grabbed my bag. Then, glancing around to see that

232

no one was watching, I made my way around the back of the school building.

I looked through the window into our classroom.

Miss Tysoe was sitting at her desk, Lazlo's note in front of her. Deep in thought, she was turning the purple sunglasses in her hand.

I had been watching her for a few seconds when she slowly raised her head and stared at me. It was as if at that moment somehow she knew that I would be there, that she understood everything that had happened, but was never going to ask how or why, or even mention it again. For ten, fifteen seconds, neither of us looked away.

Only when I smiled, did she seem to snap out of it, shaking her head like someone waking from a dream. She stood up, once more the Miss Tysoe I knew from class.

I turned from the window and walked around the building. Then, seeing my parents standing together at the school gate, I broke into a run.

## A selected list of titles available from
## Macmillan Children's Books

The prices shown below are correct at the time of going to press. However, Macmillan Publishers reserves the right to show new retail prices on covers, which may differ from those previously advertised.

**Terence Blacker**

| | | |
|---|---|---|
| Boy2Girl | 978-0-330-41503-3 | £5.99 |
| ParentSwap | 978-0-330-43741-7 | £5.99 |
| The Angel Factory | 978-0-330-48024-6 | £4.99 |
| Homebird | 978-0-330-39798-8 | £4.99 |

All Pan Macmillan titles can be ordered from our website, www.panmacmillan.com, or from your local bookshop and are also available by post from:

**Bookpost, PO Box 29, Douglas, Isle of Man IM99 1BQ**

Credit cards accepted. For details:
Telephone: 01624 677237
Fax: 01624 670923
E-mail: bookshop@enterprise.net
www.bookpost.co.uk

**Free postage and packing in the United Kingdom**